THE DEADEST ANGEL
IN BELOIT

A Jeremy and Dez
Mystery

Tom McBride

*Dedicated to Professor
George Williams, Jr. of
Beloit College:*

*Fine Educator, Brilliant
Artist, and
Solid Citizen of Beloit,
Wisconsin*

"You've got to kiss an angel good morning, and love her like the devil when you get back home." –Charlie Pride

"Our mission...is to promote a unique and personal experience that stimulates and enriches the human experience." –The Beloit, Wisconsin Angel Museum

"I hope to help the fly find its way out of the bottle." –Ludwig Wittgenstein

Table of Contents

1: Red On Powder Blue 11

2: The Downed Angel 20

3: Conversing Among Chrysanthemums 27

4: General Betrayal Is a Close Friend of Mine 33

5: Dez Takes the Case 42

6: 5512 Credibility Avenue 48

7: Tree-Barking 57

8: D.A.G. 64

9: Medieval Times 75

10: Dialing Up the Hour of Demise 80

11: A Paradox—Not Too Red & Not Too Wet 86

12: Sinner Jerry and Pastor Jimmy 92

13: Estelle's Universal Law   99

14: Oh, God!   107

15: A Stolen Raven   112

16: A Stroll Through Downtown River City   119

17: Brothers   129

18: The One Syllable Queen of Tupperware   140

19: The Distinct Possibility of Physics   149

20: Cham & Gin   159

21: Will Curiosity Kill the Cop?   165

22: A Celebratory Visit to Roscoe, Illinois 170

23: An Idiot's Summary 177

24: No Heroes Allowed   185

List of Characters

Sergeant Jeremy Dropsky *is a detective in the Beloit, Wisconsin Police Department. He is brilliant but bumbling, insightful but neurotic. He is cat-obsessed and addicted to Wittgenstein the philosopher, whom he misunderstands. He is bereft, a victim of unreturned love.*

Sergeant Abe Woodruff *is Jeremy's new partner in the police force. Also a detective, he is as honest as Jeremy's previous partner was treacherous. He walks awkwardly, runs fast, packs a quick wit and quick Glock, and enjoys his beautiful wife, whom Jeremy finds puzzling.*

Dez *is Jeremy's female orange tabby cat and his strange alter-ego. She inspires Jeremy with his best, if wackiest, ideas.*

Elizabeth Woodruff *is Abe's enigmatic (to Jeremy) wife. She is small and beautiful, with* classically restrained features and a habit of being as clear to Abe as she is opaque to Jeremy.

Charlie Baxter is the chief of detectives. He is a tall, sallow, decaying man, almost a self-described martyr as he must put up with the weird methods of Jeremy and the breezy humor of Abe.

Jonathan Bryce is a corpse, found dead in front of Beloit's Angel Museum in a bloodied powder blue suit.

Skip Bryce is a local Beloit insurance agent. He owns his own small company and was for years the runt of his family, oft victimized by Jonathan, whom he is suspected of murdering.

Margaret Bryce is Jonathan's estranged wife. She now lives in a McMansion, furnished by IKEA, in Barrington, Illinois, where she seems to display an odd blend of wholesome habits and exotic desires.

Jacob Abernathy is Margaret's gardener and handyman. He is a career jailbird whom Margaret seems to like...a lot. He and Margaret are likewise good suspects in Jonathan's murder.

Joseph and Estelle Cupps are residents of Janesville's Columbus Circle neighborhood. Joe is an affably besieged spouse, while Estelle lays down daffy universal laws. They come to be involved in a rather bizarre alibi (or non-alibi) for Skip Bryce.

Ellis Duvall is a former high school football coach and interfering citizen.

Pastor Jimmy is a self-righteous nut job and consumer advocate calmed down by Abe, who knows him from church circles.

Sinner Jerry is a dodgy used-car salesman and the target of Pastor Jimmy's ire.

Wilma Riddlehauer is Jeremy's old philosophy professor at Beloit College, from which he dropped out. She and Jeremy continue to meet from time to time, when she corrects his misreading of Wittgenstein but also helps Jeremy clarify his thinking about murder cases.

Roger Webb is Jeremy's old partner, who betrayed him by setting up a homicide and making it look legal in order to steal the victim's wife.

Frank Bunting is another corpse, not found by the Angel Museum but behind the garish Paramount Theater in Aurora, Illinois.

Arthur Simpson is a manager and substitute bartender at the Beloit Inn bar and a central if unwitting witness.

Rose and Susan Harter are feuding half-sisters. Rose is executive assistant at the Beloit Police Department, while Susan, disabled, lives in their apartment on Prairie Avenue and plots ways to annoy Rose even further.

Jerry Ricciardi is a suspected hit man living in Roscoe, Illinois.

Howard Wynn is the rotund pastor of Abe and Elizabeth's church. He preaches on the nobility and utility of love, sweet love.

Mary Webb is the ex-wife of Jeremy's mendacious and murderous partner Roger. She is also the love of Jeremy's life. Jeremy is not the love of Mary's life.

Roy Beasley is the associate pastor of Abe and Elizabeth's church. He is tall, short-haired, and oleaginous. He is the love of Mary's life.

1: Blood Red on Powder Blue

"Man down," said Charlie Baxter on the telephone at precisely 6 A.M.

It was as though Charlie—he's also called Chief of Detectives Baxter—was waiting until the clock turned 6 to ring me at home. Later I concluded the exactitude of the hour was just a coincidence. But you never know with Charlie, the ramrod cop, with salt and pepper follicles on top (more on the left than on the right), who seems to be posing for his memorial statue all the time.

A memorial statue of Charlie Baxter? Not a chance. Where would they put it—in the middle of Suds's Tavern? Charlie hung out there in off hours as often as the pictures of Irish pastoal on the walls, and the pictures on the walls never come down.

"OK," I said through the scratchy particles of sleep in my blue gray eyes. "Where?"

"You're not going to believe this, Jeremy. It's right in front of the Angel Museum."

Dez, my orange tabby, always scatters when the phone jangles. She's learning a fast return to tranquility these days. By this time she was next to me on the bed again. Suddenly she looked no longer cute but had the face of a quizzical mountain lion.

I couldn't blame her. "The Angel Museum?"

"That's correct, Sergeant Dropsky. And I think you and Abe had better get down here. I'm calling him next. Elizabeth will kill me for waking them both up early. I don't care. Line of duty, Jeremy...line of duty."

"Yeah, Charlie, right. But you're saying there's a dead man on the, uh, sidewalk in front of the Angel Museum on Pleasant Street, right?"

"That's what I'm saying."

"This is the same museum that's right across from placid Beloit College."

"That's correct, Sergeant."

"So right across from this distinguished seat of learning and civilization, and right in front of a building dedicated to angelic hosts, there is this dead person?"

"Man."

"Man. Right. Now is there any early indication of how this man came to join the non-existent?"

"Those two years at Beloit College, the seat of whatever you called it, have ruined you, Jeremy. The guy's dead. If you want to know more about it, I suggest you get your carcass down here. ASAP."

"Yes, Charlie. I guess my curiosity will get the better of me, and my wish for a regular paycheck, and so I will head to Pleasant Street and be there in fifteen minutes."

I turned to Dez. She's started to like dry food from a plastic container, and it's my very own mix. Call it dry food cat salad. I've got every kind of dry pellet assembled at random in this thing, and I shake it up to give it yet another mélange of flavors, and medley of gustatory paradise, and I pour out a few handfuls and drop it on the bed for her. She's far more eager to dine on this stuff than I am to visit the Angel Museum and inspect a body that, for all I know, had a heart attack because he was so excited about seeing Oprah Winfrey's black angel figurines. But then that made no logical sense at all, since the museum was closed all night.

Ah, I knew: He died of cardiac arrest just in *anticipation* of seeing Oprah's ceramics collection of African-themed seraphim and cherubim.

This was all horse puck. The truth is, I didn't want to go down there. It was early. I had no time for coffee or a Pop Tart. I resisted the whole idea that this required police intervention. The guy died of natural causes. How he got to go into that dark night in front of the Angel Museum: well, I put that down to coincidence.

In the course of this investigation, which I'm going to tell you about, I put down the Angel Museum link to so many damned things I've lost count.

I hopped into the little blue Mazda after telling Dez that she should stay in for the day—it was raining—and that I would be back soon because, hey, starting early I would deserve some extra time off and I'd get home and tell Dez all about the man who'd had a stroke while ceramic angels sang him to his infinite rest. Dez doesn't say much, but her stare alone tells you she's taking it all in.

When I was at Beloit College I studied the philosopher Wittgenstein with Professor Wilma Riddlehauer, and Wittgenstein said, "if a lion could talk we could not understand it." The same goes for cats, and the same goes for Dez. But old Ludwig Wittgenstein never said cats and lions couldn't understand *us*.

I'm a police detective in Beloit, Wisconsin, where we've got stuff that nobody else does, and this includes the Angel Museum in front of which this dead guy was found. Out towards Milwaukee we've got a chiropractor's office shaped like vertebrae. We've got one underground house out near Turtle Creek. We've got a railroad bridge that no train has ever been on—it's a public sculpture. And now we've got us yet another corpse.

When I got to that section of Pleasant Avenue, just north of downtown, my fellow coppers (uniform version) had it blocked off. There weren't many cars at that hour, but what cars there were the uniforms had sent looping around the blockade. There was an ambulance and a coroner. Gladys Earl, our leading crime technician (in charge of prints, DNA, smudges, and molecules) had already arrived, petite with auburn curls and wearing informal early morning jeans, fashionably faded in off-white streaks. Here the lab crew, likewise rousted out of bed, didn't have a stich of white on and looked as though they were working in a sea of syrup. They looked like they'd just finished with the body and found whatever they could for the time being. Charlie was standing as usual, straight and emaciated and tall, in an overcoat. Momentarily I found he had no tie on—just a shirt and trousers. Little drops of rain had glistened his head, and it looked at first like he'd been crying. Charlie didn't look good. The buttered rum and the sorrows of widowhood had told on him, like a tattle-tale in fifth grade informing the teacher that little Charlie has been sniffing glue again. When I see Charlie these days I feel like I've discovered something I shouldn't know about. The man is in decline.

The paradox is that a man's death would cheer him up; take his mind off life; give him something to do.

"Glad you could join us, Jeremy."

"Glad to be here, Charlie. So what did this gentleman under the tarp die of?"

"Look for yourself. Say, Abe didn't call you by any chance, did he?"

"No. Should he have? I left the house soon after you rang me."

"Forget it. He'll be here. Now lift that tarp, Jeremy."

I did. A sallow man with thinning hair and a cleft chin lay with his eyes having decently been closed, presumably by the coroner. He had on a lovely powder blue suit. At the top of the soft colored coat was a profoundly impolite splotch of red. It was as though somebody had moved into the home of one of the rich folks on Emerson Street, just east of Milwaukee Road, found some beautifully subtle and pricey slate blue wallpaper, and squirted a goodly portion of Heinz ketchup on it. You might say, even, that this would tend to spoil the effect.

And the dried Rorschach of blood didn't do a lot to improve Mr. Sallow's powder blue suit either. He was damp because it had rained off and on overnight, but at the moment nary a drop descended from the heavens, so there had been no need to examine him, I guess, under a canopy. The wetness gave him a slightly mildewed effect—and this too didn't enhance the suit any.

You wished you had a can of Fabreze, but this would spoil the evidence.

"This man's been shot to death!"

"I believe you deserve an A plus from the Police Academy, Jeremy. OK. Here's Abe."

I'd lost my previous partner under less than ideal circumstances to Aurora, Illinois. We'll get back to that later. So I needed a new partner, and we hired Abe Woodruff from Urbana, Illinois. He'd worked first at the U of I security force and then went on up to the third-in-line detective for the city of Urbana itself.

Look, since I did study philosophy at Beloit College I'm allowed to speak about the split between mind and body. And so it is with Abe. He's a seventy-four-and-a-half inch black guy who walks stiffly and uncertainly, which is a nice way of saying that Abe can't walk worth a shit. We make a good team. I am the Boy of Dough. He is the Man of Steel. Sometimes he ambles along as though walking is sort of new to him. Then you meet him, and he who is ambiguously locomotive on his feet is a broken-field runner with his tongue. There's no faster wit in Beloit than Sergeant Abe Woodruff. He once told me that he could run a 5 second forty in his youth. I believe him.

My previous partner Roger Webb cheated on, and didn't love, his wife. Abe and Elizabeth form a devoted couple. Roger in his social life couldn't walk normal. Abe can't walk normal—except in his social life. I needed normal. I liked and wanted Abe. I'm too screwed up myself to have a screwy partner.

But now Abe needed to see what I had seen; what Charlie had seen when he called me and made Dez scramble just five minutes prior to her potpourri dry cat food treat.

Abe was going to see homicide at the Angel Museum.

He looked. "Who is this sucker and how did he get himself plugged in front of a bunch of angels?" These were my thoughts, exactly. Abe went on, "I shall pray for this man on Sunday. But first I'd like to have a name just so God will know who I'm talking about."

It was mid-September; still warm enough, but you knew summer was over, and this dark drizzle was a superb down payment for coming January. Well, at least our corpse wouldn't have to shovel this year, except maybe as a zombie.

Abe got up from his crouch. He shuffled over my way. "Jer, it looks like we got our work cut out for us. What's the ID situation on this sad man?"

Charlie: "You want a name for your prayers, Abe? Well, it's Jonathan Pulford Bryce. He's got an Illinois driver's license and some credit cards and an insurance card and nothing else. But yeah, we have a name. We have a name to run."

"Lord, forgive Mr. Bryce all his sins," said Abe.

"Don't you think you should pray for his killer, too?"

"Sergeant Dropsky, as soon as we know who that is, I intend to do just that. And you should, too."

"Not me, Abe. God's been ignoring me ever since I dropped out of Beloit College."

"Now why would God do that?"

"Because God knows it used to be a religious school, and God's still hoping it will be again. He thought I could help. But then I left."

"Jeremy, I'm glad to be working with you. You talk nonsense, but you're a good cop. Besides that, you've turned me on to Dove Bars."

"I hope you guys are as happy as you are now when you're trying to solve this goddamned thing," said Charlie Baxter. "I sort of doubt it."

The rain started to pour. We all headed for the porch of the not-yet-opened Angel Museum. It was too small for such a congregation of tech people, uniforms, and august sleuths like me and Baxter and Woodruff. The EMS guy and gal, upon the advent of the unexpected downpour, hurried the corpse into the back of the ambulance. There it would stay for a while, so safe that not a drop of water could touch it. Lucky him.

2: The Downed Angel

After five minutes of heavenly drops so dense you couldn't see across Pleasant Street, the storm switched to first gear and through the leftover wetness we left the Angel Museum porch for our vehicles. The ambulance drove away with the very expired Mr. J.P. Bryce. The museum porch looked bare without all the overcrowded coppers there. The whole scene was pretty dank and low. It was just a little past 7 and River City was just coming to life.

We agreed to meet at 9 in the so-called Predicament Room over at headquarters We'd pool our information and decide what to do next. By then the "clothed-eye" folks, my weird nickname for the scene of crime techs, could give us a prelim.

I went home to cogitate, have a cup of instant, and send a Pop Tart down the hatch. Dez was sitting on the kitchen table glaring at me. She wasn't in a forgiving mood. She likes morning routines and seems to hew to them as sacred rites. This one she'd seen disrupted. So I told her that not a thing had really changed. We'd just start the morning anew as though nothing rare had happened.

I told Dez we'd found a victim down by the Angel Museum. I can't be sure, but I think she goes over there a lot. To be sure, it's over a mile to get there from the far west side, but my orange tabby is resourceful. How she gets in, I can't be sure, but any open door, however transient the breach, is game for Dez to sneak by. Now you'd think they'd toss her out. There you'd be wrong, quite wrong.

Beloit's Angel Museum is a place dedicated to nobility, inspiration, and goodness, and all three of those are insurance against tossing cats out into the cold, or even into the heat. So I'm sure they've put up with Dez at the museum. She's hopped and climbed onto the full collection, which includes angels less than an inch tall to full-sized ones. An oversized angel would be bigger than the museum itself. Dez has seen the angelic hosts from Japan and Russia, China and Slovenia. She's sniffed about Oprah Winfrey's 600 black angels, a gift to the museum, or maybe it's just a loan. I can't recall, and Dez doesn't plan to say.

Anyhow, Dez knew the Angel Museum as well as the back of her paw. So I'm pretty sure she was eager to learn about poor Mr. Bryce, whoever he was. Dez knows that I'm a good cop but with a tendency to overanalyze a little now and then. So the first thing that came to my mind once I got home with the succulent Taster's Choice steaming at my husky right side was that the placement of the vic was a message. Somebody was saying, "So you've always pretended to be an angel, J.P. Bryce, and thus let's see how you like being a dead one." That was it. Bryce had been a hypocrite, and hypocritical angels—pretend angels—are shot to death and left—where else—at an Angel Museum; at *the* Angel Museum. Now, Dez seemed to be saying to me between ecstatic meows at the latest tony cat food, "this could be international, not local." How many places in the world have angel museums? Maybe none other than River City, Wisconsin. So Bryce's killer could be from anywhere (Slovenia, Montenegro?) and could have killed Bryce anywhere, as long as he preserved the symbolism of dumping him at an *angel* museum.

Dez looked up at me balefully, and that, oh, sort of reminded me: Mr. Bryce was from Illinois. If he'd been from Slovenia or Gibraltar, maybe the symbolism theory would hold up. But he was local. Mr. Bryce was local, not global. So the site of the body was probably a matter of convenience, not a matter of symbolism.

That's the trouble, you see, when you're a college drop-out cop in Beloit. You always want what crime you get to be more interesting than it really is. This was far southern Wisconsin, not something out of the Da Vinci code.

Actually, before it was all over, Sergeant Abe Woodruff and I would be going back to the Da Vinci code theory, or something like it. But at that point, Dez had stopped swooning over the angelic meat from the cat food can, and when she calmed down, I calmed down. She helps me that way. I knew I had to stop theorizing and get to hard gumshoe facts. So after a few cups and several Pop Tarts I told Dez to have a good day and not to abuse her cat door privileges in the rain.

And I headed down to near the Illinois border and the cop house. I was heading straight for the Predicament

Room when two hundred fifty pound Rose Harter, who ran the place, wheeled on me in her long dress, this one festooned with cotton bales, and stared at me with a scrunched up face even fatter (and a lot more furious) than mine. "Susan did it," she said. "She keeps a little .22 in the arm of her chariot."

"Sorry, Rose. We all know you hate your disabled half-sister. But there was a lot more damage there than a wee .22 could do. We're maybe talking heavier semiautomatic here. Mr. Bryce met a big gun. Susan's in the clear. You'll have to put up with her a while longer—not that we're not always keeping an eye on her perfidious life of crime."

"Very funny, Sergeant. You're lucky. You live alone. I hate Susan, but she's two rooms away from me, max."

"Well, if she ever drives her wheel chair over ten miles an hour, we'll ticket her. Don't you worry, Rose. Anything new on the Bryce case that you've heard?"

"Nothing I've heard. You're late for the party. Abe got here five minutes ago. I think they're all waiting for you. Maybe you should exceed ten miles an hour yourself."

"Thanks, Rose. Your advice is credible, but what else is new?"

Rose was wrong. They weren't *all* waiting for me. Gladys Earl hadn't arrived, and one member of her team, Alton Cornwall, wasn't there either yet. Alton was even taller than Abe and had played hoops for Turner High. But he was too immobile to play college ball and had become a forensics guy. Of course some of the uniforms called him The Skyscraper. I like to think I'm wittier than that.

Charlie Baxter stood up as though he were a martyr about to be sent to the nearest bow-and-arrow squad. He was a sad-sucking tear-jerker, but you could tell he was excited, too. He frowned and throbbed at once. Three strings of leftover black-and-white hair crossed his speckled forehead with a certain embarrassment.

"O.K. What do we have here? We've found out that Bryce lived in downtown Chicago. He has a brother here in Beloit. The dead man is Jonathan. The living brother is William, though they call him "Skippy" or "Skip" around here. It didn't take us long to find this out in a small city. He's in insurance. The lads' parents have been dead for fifteen years. They're both in their 50s. They grew up in Beloit. Jon and Skip went their separate ways. Skip decided to open his own insurance biz. Jon we're not so sure about. But the address is downtown Chicago. You need money to live there. So Jon did something lucrative, or so it would seem. What was he doing in Beloit? We've got to check out Skip right away. Uniform is working on that. Skip is automatically a person of interest. Brothers kill brothers."

"You got that right, Brother!" Everyone snickered at Abe Woodruff's quip at Charlie Baxter's expense.

"Very funny, Abe. We'll get you on cable yet."

"Thanks, Brother Charlie.." Muted giggles rose again and died at once.

"What do we have on ballistics, Gladys?" Frazzled, she'd just barged in.

Gladys Earl never failed to accompany her formal reports with piercing eyes and contralto voice. The eyes asked if you were really listening, and the voice was wondering if you'd have the guts to contradict her. "Looks like the fiendish work of a Raven .25 handgun, Charlie. I'd say a sufficient part of a clip went into our man. He's pretty beat up inside. Probably dead for about 12 hours, Dr. Summers says, when a trucker going south on Pleasant spotted him around 5:30 A.M. When you looked at that one red splotch on his light blue suit, it seemed like just one bullet. When the medicos got him in the buff on the table they found a couple of other wounds, one ankle and one upper thigh. But it was the one through the heart that did for him. Our guess is that the first two did minimal damage, so the shooter decided to aim higher and got the desired results. Then there's the question, though this isn't our department, of where the deed took place and did anybody hear the shots in the early evening daylight. We can't rule out a silencer."

"That's why he was left at the Angel Museum: because the shooter was inspired by flights of angels to aim higher."

"Between you, Jeremy, and Chris Rock Woodruff here we've got laughs to go around. You'd never know we were dealing with a homicide here."

"Sorry, Charlie. I'm trying to keep up with Abe. But if he's Chris Rock, I'm Chris Farley."

"Chris Farley is dead, Jeremy."

"Don't I know it, Charlie."

Charlie Baxter: "All right. We get Skip Bryce in here ASAP. We've traced Jon Bryce's phone number—ground phone—in Chicago. We've called it. We get voice mail. We don't have a record of him living with anybody. We think he never married. But we'll find out. Priority Number One: Find out what Skip Bryce knows about why his brother was in Beloit. Let's hope he was killed here. If he was moved here we got a whole other set of problems. We also need to break the bad news to this Skip, unless he already knows because he's the proud owner of a Raven .25, maybe complete with silencer. Scene of Crime folks will continue to look for leads and subatomic particles. Abe and Jeremy: get ready to interview Skip Bryce."

So my partner and I are getting ready to talk to a suspect named Skip. And to think that some people believe I'm crazy because I talk to a cat named Dez.

3: Conversing Among Chrysanthemums

So once again it was time for Abe and me to have our traditional pre-investigation confab, and we'd agreed over the past couple of years of working together that if weather permitted we'd drive over to the college and sit in the Poetry Garden at College and Bushnell. We'd have never done it this time except for the fact that the rain decided to bother someone else (Madison, I hope). The sun came out like a fever. After the gloom there was a glare everywhere. We managed to get past Rose with only minimal chat about her spite of Susan—Abe said he'd pray for them both—and got into my pokey Mazda. By the time we got to the Poetry Garden the yellow chrysanthemums were still dripping with the sweat of the shower.

Neither Abe nor I are nature lovers, and Abe has always found the Poetry Garden a joke—"too many picnic tables for a garden and not a poem in sight that I can see, Brother Jer." But even a weird duck like me, and a normal mammal like Abe, can find some pleasure in festive plants. Besides, yeah, we admit it: we think the flowers help us think. If there's any scientific evidence to the contrary, I don't want to hear it. Abe's a smoker sometimes—he likes to say, with all the restrictions, that he "commits" smoking—and nobody is going to bother him doing so in the Beloit College Poetry Garden.

"I'm bringing my weeds to the mums, Sergeant Dropsky."

"Why am I not surprised? All right. What's the thing that strikes you most strange?"

"Easy. Whoever shot this guy didn't bother to take his wallet away."

"Right. So we found out who he was right away. So what's your line here, Abe—that this wasn't robbery or what?"

"That the perp didn't care if we found out who the victim was."

"Yeah, OK, but look: the perp might have known that we'd find out eventually, so why bother doing something that would only slow us up 48 hours?"

"And?"

"Well, I'm thinking out loud here, Abe."

"Could you lower your voice? That chrysanthemum over there looks disturbed."

"Only Dez gets to look disturbed among the lower life forms, Sergeant Woodruff."

"That cat. You got me, Sergeant. So anything else you got to say on the wallet being left on the vic?"

"Yeah: that the perp wanted us to know right away who his or her victim was."

"So you're saying this Raven hand job was fired in the heat of passion."

"I am."

"We look at the vic's brother. They should have him for us down at headquarters by late morning, early afternoon. He runs a local insurance company, over where a flower shop used to be, they say. He won't be hard to track, unless he's dead, too, in which case we might have to wonder who is out to whack the Bryce Bros."

"I doubt if we'll find him dead."

"If, Jeremy, this is heat-of-passion stuff the living bro will be suspect numero uno."

"You know, Abe, we're making a big mistake here."

"Yeah?"

"Yeah. We're theorizing in advance of facts."

"Big words from a big man, Jeremy. Where'd you get them?"

I am a big man, but Abe has four inches on me. He's got a Roman nose—that snout is so high-arched it could be the Golden Gate Bridge—and a smile you could warm your hands on.

"Where'd I get those words, Sergeant Woodruff? I received them from none other than Sherlock Holmes, a better detective than either of us. And yes, you are very correct, sir. I am a big man, with a flabby square face and a round body. I am a paradox. I square the circle. Throw in my close-cropped hair, my contact lenses, and my widow's peak, and you've got a real handsome dude. You know, this self-description means that I'm a really good observer—sort of a Sherlock myself."

"Sherlock. Is he the dude that noticed the dog didn't bark?"

"The same, but I can't recall which story that is. Anyhow, we're dredging up theories in advance of any data. That's a capital mistake. "

"Better than capital punishment. But look, Sergeant Dropsky, Big Sir, I'm not exactly without facts here. Nearest kin are generally good suspects, and those are stats, and stats are facts."

"Got to admit you're right, Abe."

"I am right. So do we know anything about why Skip would have hated Jon enough to kill him?"

"We know nothing, but we're going to ask."

"And we start by finding out if Skip has a Raven .25 registered in his name. I've already gotten Rose to put in a request for that very information."

"Good. If you hadn't, I would have. That's vital."

Abe looked up from staring at the nearest lingering chrysanthemum. Students and faculty were walking to and fro, nearly always by themselves. Abe said, "Look at all this walking traffic. What is this, a car dealer? Ever noticed how when you're in the waiting room and getting your brakes fixed, somebody's always walking from one place to another with a sheet of paper in their hand?"

"This is not a car dealership, Abe. I used to go here. And before you ask, I never got my brakes fixed at all here."

"They got the engine going, though. I think the brothers have lived apart for a long time. That's just my impression from Baxter. Now, Beloit and Chicago: they're only 85 miles apart, but beyond that they're a zillion years apart."

"You mean that Skip and Jon have had, uh, slightly different lifestyles."

Abe smiled and showed all the ivory chairs in his dining room. "You cracked the code, Jeremy."

"Well, the parents have been dead for years, so it's a bit late for a falling out over a will. What does that leave other than general betrayal?"

"What do you mean by general betrayal, Mr. Dropsky?"

"General betrayal, Mr. Woodruff, is a catch-all term. It includes any kind of major deception."

"What would you know about it?"

"Plenty. I used to be Roger Webb's partner."

"The dude who might otherwise be called 'my predecessor?'"

"The very same. And he betrayed me once."

"I gotta tell you, Jeremy, that that's been the skinny around the station ever since I arrived. Want to open up?"

"No. A fat man should not try to talk about the skinny."

"You're a caution. Why not?"

"Because it's personal."

"Didn't he save a damsel in distress and get a promotion to Aurora, and isn't Aurora the second largest city in Illinois? Now aren't those facts, Sherlock?"

"OK, Abe. That was a while ago, and the whole case is closed. But I'll tell you, and ask you not to ask questions, that she was a damsel but she was never in distress."

"Whoa! Say more, man!"

"I will not. I decided to let it go two years back. Or maybe I should say that nobody in power was going to let me not let it go. So I bailed."

"Webb's ex-wife is a member of our church. The story is she's dating the associate pastor."

"Who is single."

"Who is single."

"I'm not surprised. Mary deserves somebody honest. I guess an associate pastor fits the bill. Here's a ping and here's a text, Abe. Skip Bryce is waiting for us. He's been there for all of five minutes, just long enough to hear Rose ask if she can take out life insurance on adorable, crippled Susan."

"Interrogating a guy named Skip," said Abe, "is not in my job description."

4: General Betrayal Is A Close Friend Of Mine

Skip Bryce was a 50-something year old Chihuahua. He was little and barky with beady eyes. He hunched down across the interview table from us like he was going to spring on us, or maybe a little like a bland but cornered rodent ready to bare his teeth. His look was wary and resentful. He reminded me of why I was glad I was living with Dez and not a wee yap dog.

This is not to say that he was guilty of anything other than a petite canine look.

But he was also a defeated man. The anger seemed more for him than for us. He was mad at somebody but not us. He was mad at himself. He snarled not to intimidate but to emote.

Well, I thought, we all have our troubles, and these things happen in life. I tried to come up with another cliché but failed.

Abe said, "First, of course, we're sorry for your loss. We need you to help us find out what happened to your brother."

"My brother. Yes, Jonathan was my brother. Well, he was my brother. You're telling me he's dead, got shot, and I'm hearing it, but I sort of don't believe it."

"Believe it," I said. "When did you last see him?" I secretly or not so secretly thought the answer might be, "Just before I pulled the trigger." That was not what I got.

"I couldn't say."

"You couldn't say?"

"Well, years and years ago. I'm still in shock. So please bear with me. In fact, I insist you bear with me, OK? You guys like precision. I have no precision. I saw Jonathan many years back, but I can't give you month or even year."

"But he was only in Chicago."

"Look, folks. Mr. Jonathan Bryce and I were estranged. Let's just say we didn't have a lot of common subject matter and leave it at that."

"We can't leave it at that. Your brother got himself murdered."

"Right, and I still can't believe that. Let me make a long story short. I hadn't seen him in years. I don't know why he was in Beloit after all these years. I'm saddened by his death, and you can knock me over with a feather when you tell me he was murdered. I'm sad about it because I wish things had been different. Your Officer Hildalgo tells me he was found in front of the Angel Museum—like some sick joke. I don't know why he came back here. I don't know who killed him. I have no idea why he was murdered. And now I wish you'd let me go away and grieve or celebrate or whatever it is I want to do. Do I need a lawyer?"

Sergeant Abe Woodruff: "If you think you're in any sort of legal trouble, you should consider hiring an attorney to represent you."

"Well, that answers it, Sergeant. I'm not in any legal trouble, so I don't plan to throw good money after a bad shyster. May I go? *Can* I go?"

"Not yet, sir," I said. "We need more detail from you. You'll think we're prying, and nothing you say leaves this room unless it becomes of legal pertinence. Much of what you tell us will seem irrelevant to you, and it might turn out to be irrelevant to our inquiry. But experience teaches that sometimes the most unimportant thing can become significant." I was proud of this little speech, which I'd perfected and given many times. Dez has heard me rehearsing it. Sometimes I pretend I'm interrogating her.

"Am I a suspect then?"

"Not really," said Abe, "or not until and unless you give us a reason to consider you one. We just need more detail."

"I feel like I'm at a funeral, and the longest-winded woman in town decides to give a memorial, and then you know you're going to be in the chapel for another twenty minutes."

Skip wore a tan seersucker shirt with the top button unfastened. He had a beige seersucker coat on. He seemed to have more hair below his Adam's apple than he had on his head. He continued to crouch at the table and lowered his head as though in battering ram position. He must have been about five six and weighed maybe 130 pounds. His eyeteeth were sharp, and he had a habit of chattering up and down on them with a little scowl.

He was harmless, in other words.

"Make that thirty minutes at least."

"What do you want to know?"

"Why you and your late brother weren't best of friends."

"Do you want the short story or the novel?"

"How about a novella?" Skip was startled to hear a cop talking this way, but remember: I had had some college.

"Well, we both got in wrong. I'm wiry and short. He was always tall and big. He was older by a couple of years. He would turn on the hose in our yard and flood the neighbor's Bermuda grass next door. This he'd do late at night. The neighbor—this was on Bluff Street where we grew up in one of the grander old homes, I guess you'd say—would get up and think he needed to build an Ark in his yard, which is a nice way ot saying he wasn't amused to find Turtle Creek flowing through his grass. And then Jonathan would say that I and my friends had done it, and I was hard-pressed as a nine year old to prove him wrong, and my parents, well, they liked the big strapping boy better, I suppose, than they liked the little piss-ant (that would be Yours Truly). Well, it went on like that. I worked odd jobs to buy myself a car as a sophomore in high school and he was a BMHS senior who put smelly cheese on the manifold so that the whole experience would be nice and ruined for me. He played tight end and caught one winning touchdown pass. He was glib and a ladies' man. I was inarticulate and timid. I was no good with girls. I'm still not, except that once."

"That once?"

"Yeah. Well, there were one or two areas where I actually excelled Jonathan. He went to Madison but dropped out of university after two years. I actually finished college, at Ripon. He was good at football but never played in college. I was a great no-hit good fielder shortstop, though I came to baseball late, and actually started on the team my senior year at Ripon. I actually played college varsity baseball. I was little and scrappy but had no fear of screaming grounders and scooped them up. I had an adequate arm. Of course my batting average was about .119—some games they even batted me behind the pitcher."

"This is interesting stuff, Mr. Bryce," said Abe, "but I thought we were talking about girls...about you and girls, to be exact."

"We were. Well, by now I hope you'll see that I mostly existed to feed Jonathan's superiority complex, to be the butt of his jokes. He was Mother and Father's clear favorite. If we'd been horses they'd have bet on him. And, like I say, he was good with women."

"Except once, when he wasn't? Could we get on with that, sir?"

"He was good with Margaret."

"Was Margaret here in Beloit? Do we have a last name for Margaret here?"

I realized as soon as I asked the question that it was insensitive. I was about to hear some sort of lovelorn story, maybe, and all I seemed to want were external facts. Mary Webb is the love of my life, and I wouldn't like someone asking me, "Does this Mary have a last name?" But it was too late.

"Margaret," growled Skip, also a little plaintively, "was at Ripon."

"And you and she were an item there?"

"An item! You make it sound like something off a grocery list. Yes, we were quite attached. I was going to ask her to marry me."

"Look, Mr. Bryce. I hate to be a bureaucrat here, but I know we have to check into this, so I have to ask you for her last name."

"Yes, you'll need to contact Margaret. Her last name was French. We were in our early twenties then. She was what you'd call a handsome woman. She had a horsey, olive-skinned, but kind face. She was a volleyball superstar. She was a big girl, probably two inches taller than I was, but of course two inches shorter than Jonathan. She was from around Chicago; grew up over near where the fancy mall is now; just north of Chicago."

"Skokie."

"That's it. Diamond-shaped face. Great mouth for kissing, or so I've speculated. Muscular. I adored her. I majored in economics, and she in Spanish. We never formally dated, but we'd meet for coffee and sometimes a beer. She could outdrink me. We were buddies, but I think— I know—she could tell it was more than that. She was really the first and only lady I ever had much luck with, and even then it was because the romance was kept out of it. Whenever you put the hearts and flowers in the ring, I was a tongue-tied mess. But Margaret and I were sneaking up on each other, and I think she was starting to love me. I was going to ask her to marry me. I told my parents this, and they got excited and interested for me. But—"

Yes?"

"They must have told Jonathan."

"Go on."

Well, the next thing I knew he showed up for a friendly visit at Ripon. He stopped by one late morning in October— I remember because we'd had a severe frost the night before and the sun was just blinding off the ice—and he asked himself to lunch with me and Margaret. And he insisted we go to an off-campus restaurant. And he insisted on paying."

"Well, Mr. Bryce," said Abe, "it's obvious you didn't marry Margaret French because our records show you've never been married, and our records are good. So are you working up to something here?"

"You could say that, Sergeant. By November Margaret had slowly but surely stopped seeing me. And that was that."

"And you trace this development to the visit of your older brother, the deceased?" And yes, my blood was running cold and hot at the same time: Brother snakes brother; brother becomes dearly departed; second brother is responsible for first brother's void of existence. I was compositing. Cops do. They shouldn't.

"I know that Jonathan broke Margaret and me up, yes."

"How do you know?"

"Too much of a coincidence otherwise. Her distance dated from his visit. I think I even know what she told him. You see, I had this best baseball buddy, a guy named David, who was a slugging first baseman. I loved that guy and spent a lot of time with him. We did stuff together. If you're shy like me, you waste a lot of time with other guys. Well, I don't know if 'waste' is right. Anyhow, David and I were best buds. And I think Jonathan told Margaret that, hey, maybe there's something not quite right about that. Jonathan always made it his business to know everything."

"But you don't know that that's what your brother told your girlfriend."

"I don't know that, and she was never, I guess, quite my girlfriend."

"And you don't know," I asked with that ah-ha tone in my voice, "that he had anything to do with the break-up. You don't know that for sure, do you, Mr. Bryce?"

"Well, I'm pretty sure."

"How so? Why?"

"Well, gentlemen, as I said, you will need to contact Margaret about my brother's murder. You see, she's no longer Margaret French. She's Margaret Bryce now, and has been for over twenty years."

Chalk up a point for General Betrayal. As Abe started liking to say, "General Betrayal is a good friend of yours, isn't he, Jeremy?"

5: *Dez Takes The Case*

Our interview rooms are, on purpose, about as antiseptic as you can get. Everything's bleached white, even the aluminum chair plastic. It's like we hear so many infected things in these rooms that we try to keep them germ-free otherwise. We've got good audio and video equipment, too; but before we got back into the Mazda, on our way to interview Skip Bryce, it had occurred to me that we should just pick him up and bring him back to the Poetry Garden for a chat. That would have been unprofessional and impossible of course.

But just as Skip gave us his mini-bombshell—that his late brother had taken his sweetheart away from him, Tennessee Waltz style—a big yellow moth dive-bombed into the east wall of the interview room. The thing had been with us the whole time, but we were trapped with it, and it with us. There's no way to open windows any longer. You need a city permit to do that. We couldn't open the door because that would ruin confidentiality policy. Abe's tall, and I think he could have stood on his chair and swatted the thing with the (so far) skinny case file. But he didn't do that. I don't know why he didn't, but my guess is that we were talking about the topic of killing with Skip, and Abe didn't want to do any more killing, even of a desperate moth. It just wouldn't be decorous. Now I've never asked Abe about this. Some things between partners should be kept away from the English language.

The moth didn't seem to bother Mr. Bryce. He said he needed to keep an appointment with a potential client who wanted house insurance for a dwelling built on a flood plain near the Rock River, and he said he was innocent and uninformed and couldn't allow his brother's surprising death to ruin his business. So we let him go, provided he return at 2 PM for more. Old Skip had been soooooooooo open with us, and maybe he thought that would clear him. It didn't. He had more motive than ever, and we needed to get into alibis. And if they worked out for him, we needed to get into hit men with a few stray Raven .25s lurking about.

DNA was sort of useless. It wasn't totally void, but the stuff is better lifted in enclosed spaces. If only the shifty Jonathan had been left dry and *inside* the Angel Museum. Then we could have compared (*they* could have compared) his DNA with that on the angel Gabriel's horn. Gladys Earl said there'd be some DNA forthcoming, but she didn't have high hopes it would tell us anything other than that Mr. Jonathan Bryce was actually Mr. Jonathan Bryce.

It was noon plus thirty, and Skip was the big focus. So while he was discussing, or so he said, flood plain coverage in Afton, where the Rock often does not flow gently, I decided to grab a Marie Callender Parmesan Cheese Chicken Pot Pie (sounds grand, doesn't it, or German, with all those adjectives), and an Orange Crush. This meant home, and home meant far west side. I got a couple of dormer windows in the front of my house, and they're one of two things that keep the place from being nothing more or less than a puke-green wooden box. I also had a porch built house-length. That's the other thing that redeems the place. You might wonder why, if I don't like the color, I don't get it painted powder blue to match, maybe, Skip Bryce's brother's suit color. Well, I don't have the money yet, but when I do we're talking Satanic red.

I went around the back and walked into the kitchen. Dez did not present herself, but the cat flap looked somehow as though it might have recently been swinging, and the sun had deigned to make a comeback, so it wasn't hard to figure that she had decided to watch an episode of her continuing life in the great out of doors.

I put chicken Marie in the micro and found a cold can of Crush in the back of the G.E. and tried to think of myself as a happy man, or at least as a contented cow. I heard a little door flap and then another one and there was Dez. She must have heard me come in. She was hungry—tell me something I don't know—so I fixed her a wet and dry kitty salad and soon enough we were in high festive mode.

I decided in fifteen minutes or so to have a catnap, which I mean literally because I'm sitting down on the bumpy turquoise couch with my eyes closed, and she's on my parking lot of a stomach. But neither of us could sleep. We were both too keyed up. And it was then that I realized: Dez had been over at Skip's insurance agency when Pedro Hidalgo arrived with the news that his get-lost brother had been shot and his powdery blue remains had been left to augment the scenery in front of the Beloit Angel Museum. And Dez was reporting that Skip asked, "Are you sure," and Pedro said he, Pedro, didn't get many things wrong.

And Skip was naturally beside himself and had to tell somebody but there was no Margaret to share the news with—she was bitter Ripon College history—so, according to Dez, he stumbled into the reception area and told his secretary. Now Skip is not the sort to have two secretaries, one for each knee, so there was very likely not a stitch of erotic fabric between him and Ms. Whatever Her Name (Dez didn't recall it).

But she would have said, "Oh, Mr. Bryce. I'm so sorry. So shocking." And Skip would have felt cross-pressured. Her words (let's call her Ms. McCall) were so trite, but somebody had spoken them, and Skip was grateful for that. He was at the core a lonesome man; and while later we'd find out that he had a few unofficial club memberships in town (poker, Rotary), he was an almost friendless man in the end. Most of his friends were friends on the road (people he'd met in the line of duty) and no one was a friend of the heart. And so Dez thought, as she watched this miserable scene of shock and maybe secret glee, Mr. Bryce (Skip) was a figure of such monumental solitude that if Ms. McCall hadn't been there with her hackneyed consolation he'd have had to hire someone to say how sorry they were.

Well, these were just Dez's impressions. She goes everywhere and sees everything, and she's stealthy, so neither Pedro nor Ms. McCall nor Skip would have noticed her lurking under the desk and gathering intelligence for me. But really: how do you take news like this if you're Skip? You're traumatized; you think he had it coming; you're shot with melancholy that two brothers came to hate each other.

What else was he thinking? That "I hope I can get away with this"? I figured, and Dez surely agreed, that even if he'd done it, the news that it had been done would still be a shock. I looked at Dez, who was washing herself. She was ignoring me and had in fact retreated to the west side of the divan. Was Dez saying, "Did he do it? Above my pay grade."

Yeah, I guess Dez is right. Abe and I will have to find out that one for ourselves. I was just grateful that Dez had been there to see the news broken. That saved me from having to ask Pedro Hidalgo for his impressions. Dez's real value is that when she skulks all over Beloit, she comes back to me not just for Meow Mix but also to give me context. Beloit is the city of broken things: hearts, brotherhood, sisterhood, and lives. When you solve crimes and keep the peace, as I'm paid to do, and as Abe is paid to do, you need to remember that you're only picking up the broken pieces. You're not mending them. You can't.

I thought about asking Dez to look in on Mary Webb to see if she really was about to marry the underling preacher at Abe's church. I thought better of it. Some privacy should not be breached. It would be creepy of me, even, to employ Dez, to spy on Mary. But I still think she and I and Dez would make a mighty fine threesome somewhere. Still, it wasn't my late brother who took her away from me. It was a pastor somewhere here in River City, home of Angel Museums and anatomically shaped chiro offices.

And she was never mine to begin with. Dez hopped up on my lap and got her face close to mine and looked downright menacing close up. She's cuter at a distance. Skip Bryce was supposed to re-join us at 2. It was 1:40.

6: 5512 Credibility Avenue

Skip Bryce, the informal but puppy-like man with the undone collar, had returned to us with his neck adorned by a black and white tie and his tiny shortstop's torso dressed in a pressed white shirt. He explained that when he'd gotten the catastrophic news he'd not been in business attire at the office because he had no appointments until around noon. Now he'd seen his client. He looked worn, as though the Chihuahua, so scrappy if innocuous before, had had too long an outing in the Gobi desert, or maybe just too long a walk with his owner in our local Leeson Park. Skip looked beat. He was tired of fighting, either reality or his brother or us. His little head was still a bit horizontal and low, but no longer as a result of a pseudo-attack position. Now his head was just low, period. What did we want to know?

Before I left the house Dez added one more thought: That among other feelings Skip had when Pedro Hidalgo paid him that fateful visit was the idea that somebody was targeting the Bryce brothers. What had they done to somebody for them to do that? So if I'm Skip Bryce, whether or not Dez is spying on me in the corner of the office, I'm a mess of relief and shock and confusion and fear and gratitude and maybe guilt. When you have that many sliders and fork balls and fast falls and changes of pace coming at you, even if you were once Ripon's starting shortstop, you're going to get beat up.

And Skip by his own admission was never a good hitter anyhow. By now he'd been beaned and was ready to pretend the interview room was intensive care. Sorry about all the baseball metaphors. I'm a big fan. No, the Brewers are not overrated this year. But they won't be in any World Series either.

"Again, fellows: do I need a lawyer? I'll admit something: I'm flattened and I can't think."

Now Sergeant Abe Woodruff is not like me. He would never think of painting his house Satanic red. In fact, his place over behind Menard's is an angelic off-white brick. Abe is a nice man, and he felt sorry for Skip. And so my answer, "That's up to you, the lawyer thing," never got mentioned. Instead, Abe said something quite different, and later I asked him why he said it, and he wasn't overly polite in his answer: "Because my people and I identify with folks who aren't guilty but need a lawyer anyhow. Why did you even have to ask, Jeremy?" Well, maybe I had that coming. Anyhow, here's what Abe said to our Skipper:

"Mr. Bryce, our job is not to find out if you did this. Our job is to find out who did this. Now if you didn't do it, you might think you don't need a lawyer. But a lawyer can be useful even for innocent folks. I'm not supposed to say this, I guess, but I figure facts will tell, whether you get a lawyer or not. If you're in the clear, you may not need a lawyer. But getting one might also, even if you're innocent, save you some difficulty along the way. It's up to you."

"I appreciate that, sir. OK. I can at least think this well: I'll tell you some more—whatever you ask—and if along the way later you're putting heat on me, I'll get an attorney. I don't think you will put the heat on me because I don't know anything about this. But I figure there's no reason to lawyer up right now when you've got nothing to conceal. So ask away."

"All right, sir," I said in my most insistent and official voice. "Here's how we work. We hear stories, and we check them against other stories. And whatever seems to be left standing after all these stories support or cancel each other is the truth, and that's what we report to the prosecution folks. Now you've told us a story about your brother, and that story tells us you didn't like him, and every now and then when people don't like each other they shoot each other. So you've got motive. Now we need to talk alibi. If you've got a solid alibi, then we start to look at guns-for-hire. We've no record that you own the type of gun that did the deed. That does not mean you don't own such a gun or that you didn't employ someone who does. But first we have to go to alibi. So your brother Jonathan met his death late afternoon or early evening yesterday. Where were you between 5 and 7?"

"On a wild goose chase, Sergeant Dropsky."

"OK. You were chasing wild geese, and people who chase wild geese can't murder their brothers at the same time. Is that what you're telling us?"

"I think this is Jeremy's funny way of asking you what you mean when you say you were chasing wild geese." I took that as a reproach from my partner, but then he's a happily married church-going man that isn't lonely and bitter like me. He's sweet, but it's easy to be sweet when you've got someone. I don't have anyone, and anyone includes Mary Webb. Dez makes me glad but not sweet.

"Well, you know what I mean. I went off on a false errand. I'd gotten a call from this woman in Janesville who wanted to talk life insurance. I'd gone over some options for her on the phone, but she didn't seem to be taking them in. She wanted to insure herself. She'd called a couple of times, and every time was less productive than the previous one. So I told her we needed to talk face-to-face. She said fine, and that her hubby would be there, and he could help her understand, and so the three of us would go over possibilities and price structures, and then, just maybe, at the end of this nice visit I'd make a good sale. So off I went in my car up north, and this was between around 4:45 and 6:45 before the whole thing was finished."

As I said before, Skip had his office where a flower shop used to be. One of these days I'm going to send Dez back down there to see if there are any left over flower pots in the back. I'm always looking for freebees. This is something I don't necessarily like about my life: that I'm always thinking the world owes me something, anything, for free. It's part of my general grumpiness. For now, though, I imagined Skip leaving the former emporium of floral delights and getting into his late model gray Taurus, steering the vehicle onto Pleasant Avenue, driving right by the Angel Museum (with no thought of his brother?), and traveling to Wisconsin's Park City, our haughty neighbor to the north, which makes outlandish claims about the amount of public greenery in the city.

"This is good, Mr. Bryce," said Abe. "We just need the name and address of this woman in Janesville, and we've at least got your personal alibi out of the way." Abe was really trying to be helpful, but that was OK because we both knew that the facts would lead to where they would whether we were encouraging to old Skip or not.

"I can't give you her name and address."

"You can't—but why? Why can't you? Didn't you go there?"

"I went there. I know the woman had told me on the phone that her name was Gloria Warren, and she said her address was 5512 Columbus Circle. I don't have a phone number. She called the office and not my cell phone. I never wrote her number down. The first conversation was confusing, like I said, so I saw nothing in it until she called back one late afternoon about a week ago. This one was a mess, too, but then she said I could drive up there and meet her and her husband. When she mentioned the husband, I thought maybe he was a lot less loopy than she seemed to be. Anyhow, I never wrote down or asked for a phone number. It just didn't seem that promising. But I was willing to talk face-to-face provided this third party was present. And she said he would be. I have no phone number. I didn't think I needed it anyhow. You see, it was either 'this woman is not tracking, so what's the use' or 'once I get to Janesville and talk to hubby in person I'll make a possible sale.' A phone number wasn't in the cards. So I just drove up there."

"Well, OK. So you didn't get the number. You don't have a number. But you have an address. We have an address. Believe it or not, Mr. Bryce, I even wrote it down: 5512 Columbus Circle, Janesville; Gloria Warren. Shouldn't be hard to check. Seregeant Woodruff and I are really good checkers, too."

"Yes, but you can't check."

"Oh, yes, we can. As I said, we're really good at it: world-class checkers."

"Well, you see, I knew where Columbus Circle was in Janesville. One of my Ripon classmates even lived there once, bless his soul. I visited him. I knew where this area of Janesville was. I was even looking forward to being up in that neighborhood again—that and a sale were part of the attraction. The area has these three little parks and a long circular street and lots of neat houses, all styles."

"Well, the whole city, "I said, "calls itself Wisconsin's Park Place or something like that. And it's getting on towards winter, and I can see that you'd want to take in as much green as possible, Mr. Bryce. But Sergeant Woodruff and I have no interest in your love of nature. Well, I won't say no interest at all, but it's more of an interest we'd take after work. Now we're at work. So we need to check out 5512 Columbus Circle and Mrs. Gloria Warren, whether she can fathom life insurance or can't fathom life insurance. In fact, even if she couldn't fathom any variety of insurance we'd still need to check out your whereabouts. This is, as they like to say on British TV, a murder inquiry."

"But," said Skip, "there is no 5512 Columbus Circle. I never found the place. I drove around that circle three or four times and never found it. I stopped a couple of people on Court Street and on Garfield Street and asked them. They had no idea. I got frustrated and parked by one of the little parks. They've got a Little Library box there in one of them. I didn't know that. Anyhow, I needed to cool my jets. This had been a con job, on me. There was no 5512 Columbus Circle. I'd been misled. I drove back to Beloit."

"And this was between a quarter of 5 and a quarter of 7?"

"About that, yeah."

"So while your brother got himself shot somewhere—we don't know where yet—you were looking for a non-existent address in Janesville in order to sell Mrs. Gloria Warren and her husband life insurance. That's your tale, right?"

"My tale?"

"Sorry, your account. Your statement. Your testimony. I don't think we want to have this written up for you to sign yet," I said. "I think we need to verify it first."

"You say you asked a couple of people on nearby streets," said Abe. "Can you remember them? Was there anything unusual about them, something that would help us identify them so we an ask them if they saw you and tried to help you, even though they couldn't?"

"Not really, no. For example, they didn't have a dog with them. One was a man and the other was a woman. I was too ticked off to notice much about them."

"Nothing? Not even whether they were long or short, green or purple?"

"I think Sergeant Dropsky is saying that without details this is going to be hard to verify. And, sir, we need to verify it or you may be needing a lawyer after all. Now of course we can try to check phone records of calls to your office, and we can get a court order for that or you can give us your permission. I don't know what they might reveal."

"Well, there is no 5512 Columbus Circle. What else can I say?"

"If this woman calls back to ask where the Hell you were, make sure you get a phone number, OK? It will help us, and above all it will help you."

"I can't think any more. Jon shot dead; for some reason in Beloit; wild goose chase in Janesville. Has God turned against me?"

"God is Sergeant Woodruff's department, Mr. Bryce. Do you think you could have written the address down wrong?"

"No, I know I did not."

"That's a point in your favor," said Abe. "If you'd said you did, then we might think that's a convenient answer. You say you didn't. This gives your story credibility. I've got to say that. But getting the whole account credible is going to take some doing. Then again, as Jeremy here says, we're first-class checkers."

"We're first-class checkers," I said, "but we have a long drive before we get you, Mr. Bryce, to 5512 Credibility Avenue."

7: Tree-Barking

"Dude sure had a raspy voice," said Abe.

"Well," I said, "he did at the end. I don't know so much about the beginning. He had a creepy walk, though."

"Only at the end, Brother," said Abe.

"So why don't you gentlemen tell me what you really think? I won't reveal it," said Elizabeth Woodruff, a petite third-grade teacher in the Beloit school system and Abe's spouse. We were sitting in their ranch-style home behind Menard's and Wal-Mart. Abe has a nicer house than I do, but then Elizabeth earns a salary. Dez does not.

She (Elizabeth, not Dez), has a long pony tail and a pleasing gait, quite unlike Abe's graceless shuffle. Abe grins from left anvil to right stirrup. Elizabeth's smile is a Mona Lisa job, your standard riddling one-third grin. I never know if she's encouraging me or mocking me or encouraging me so she can mock me.

Abe and Elizabeth had invited me over for coffee and lemon meringue pie. It was the evening of the second day of the inquiry. I think they felt sorry for me. Maybe they really like me. Anyhow, I'm a most reliable pie-hole.

A silver coffee pot and earthtone mugs sat on a faux marble coffee table. The pie, now rather decimated, was in a round glass dish. The coffee table would have looked phony in my house. In theirs it looked elegant, but that's because they have a home to live in while I just have a house to sleep in.

"I believe the man," said Abe. "The story's too crazy to make up."

By this time Janesville police had started to distribute flyers in the neighborhood around Columbus Circle: HAVE YOU SEEN THIS MAN? along with a photo of Skip. We'd had to get Skip's permission to do this, and he didn't like the notoriety. But it was Janesville, not Beloit, and his name wasn't on the flyer, and it stated plainly that he was not wanted for any crime. We'd talked to Janesville police, and they weren't going to go door-to-door (too much work and too few cops), so the flyer was the only option left for now, and we hoped we wouldn't have to ask Skip if he minded expanding the flyer to the Janesville paper. So far we hadn't a nibble, though these were early days. But here was Abe saying he found Skip credible.

"What about you, Jeremy?" Elizabeth smiled at me in encouragement as though to hope that I too had a lot of faith in humankind.

"I'm not sure of course. But I have less faith in the man than Brother Woodruff does."

"That's because there isn't enough Lord Jesus in your life, Sergeant Dropsky."

"Well, that's not true, Sergeant Woodruff. If Jesus told me he'd tried to sell life insurance to a non-existent crazy woman in Janesville, Wisconsin, I'd have believed him.

Skip's phone logs on the days he identified as relevant do contain a couple of odd numbers, both traceable to phone cards, and you know as well as I do that it's going to take a week to find the actual number the calls were dialed from. But if Jesus had gotten calls made through phone cards, I'd have believed Him."

"Well, Jeremy," said Elizabeth. "Now we're making progress here."

I thought: I'd go to church with them if Dez could come along.

What a day it had been! In the early afternoon, after Abe and I had gotten back from making arrangements in Janesville, my cell phone did its arpeggio chimes, and there was Ellis Duvall at the other end. Ell was the retired BMHS football coach, a legend in his own mind.

"Jeremy? Ellis Duvall here. Say, this is not my business, but I've read and heard about Skip Bryce's brother. I know you're talking to Skip. Let me just say, Skip had nothing to do with any of this. You're barking up the wrong tree here, you and Abe."

"Yeah, Ell, but it's a tree we have to bark up. Woof Woof!"

"What's that? Oh, I see what you're saying. Yeah, you have to check everything out. But Skip's not your man. I'm just saying."

"How do you know Skip, Coach?"

"Skip? I know him through the football boosters club. Skip was there whether we won or lost."

"OK, but, well, Ell, what does that have to do with it?"

"Well, you know how it is, Jeremy. A man who isn't a fair weather fan is an honest man."

"And honest men don't kill their brothers."

"Something like that."

"OK, Coach, this is noted. Thanks for letting us know...what you think."

"That's what a good citizen is for, Sergeant."

"And good citizens don't kill their brothers either, right? Do you have a brother, Coach?"

"No."

"Well, you're in the clear on that score anyhow. Thanks for calling."

Sometimes I drive down to a junkyard in South Beloit and park and say, "This is my life."

And then of course there was the even-heftier-than-I Rose, whom you couldn't get by without having to hear about her latest dust-up with Susan, her roommate and half-sister and the object d'art of her eternal hatred as the two of them disputed over which of them their late father loved more. I've always thought—and have told Abe—that we ought to arrest Susan, wheel her into a holding cell for a day, show her sitting there to Rose, release her the next day, and hope that Rose is satisfied that we've done *something* and will stop bothering us about the subject.

"Nah," said Abe. "Elizabeth and I will try to get our pastor to counsel them."

Since then, I ask Abe every week or so when he and Elizabeth are going to do this. He always answers the same: "Any year now, Brother Jer. Any year."

Ellis, Rose, Janesville flyers, lemon meringue pie, black coffee: and that's the way it was on September 17, 2017. And Abe and I are so reduced by the poverty of helpful facts in this case that when I say Jesus Christ probably didn't do it, that represented real progress.

"What I can't get over, Abe and Elizabeth, is that as yet there's no reliable phone record of this so-called call. How likely is that? Skip didn't write it down. He didn't take it on his cell phone. I'm sorry, folks, but it's like Skip wanted this alibi woman to vanish so we couldn't check the alibi itself."

"Yeah, but we got no record that he's ever owned a gun. And if we're talking hit man, he has no need for an alibi."

"We got no *record* that he owns a gun. In fact, the records show that he does not own a gun. But the records won't show whether or not he *has* a gun."

"Agreed, Brother. But then if he has a secret gun, that's his program for deceiving us. He has no need to give us this crazy story about the lady in Janesville."

"No, Abe. He could do both. He could be doing a real flimflam job on us."

"You act like this guy is some master criminal," said Elizabeth. "Is he?"

"Well, Elizabeth. You mean could we really have a master criminal here in Beloit, River City? Don't sell Beloit short. A world-famous explorer came from here. These extraordinary things can happen, even here."

"What world-famous explorer?"

"Roy Chapman Andrews."

"Oh, him," said Elizabeth. "Well, Abe and I never heard of him before we moved here. That's how world-famous he is. And now you're saying Beloit is home to the world-famous master criminal Skip Bryce."

"Look, you two: you and I can believe what we want, but until we get this alibi nailed down, Skip Bryce is suspect numero uno. I don't want us to get sidetracked here, OK? Skip seems credible—his story is too nuts not to be—and we can't prove otherwise, so naturally we move on to some other suspect just to think we're getting somewhere, and we wait a week or two for some tech in Los Angeles or Denver to try to trace those phone card calls. With old Skip as the most obvious suspect, that could be a real time-waster. But we do have to talk to the woman that ditched Skip for the late great Jonathan, and tomorrow we're heading to Barrington, Land of Lincoln, to do just that. I'd like to know why Jon was living in Chicago while Magnificent Margaret is living in a far northwest suburb. They were presumably separated. She can tell us about her apparently alienated husband's life and whether or not she knows anything about Skip and Jon's latest relationship, if any. We need to keep gathering data. But Skip is a first-rate chief suspect, and we can't forget that."

"And one other thing," said Abe.

"Which is?"

"Which is that Ms. Margaret herself might have done it."

"Now who's the cynic?"

"A woman named Magnificent Margaret," said Elizabeth, "is exactly the type to leave her bastard husband's body in front of an angel museum."

"Such talk, Elizabeth—and you and Abe want me to go to church with you?"

"Would you like another piece of pie, Jeremy?"

"I would. Thought you'd never ask."

"If we solve this," said Abe, "let's celebrate right here at our place with some angel food cake."

8: D.A.G.

On the way to Barrington next day Abe did most of the talking, and I did all of the driving. He'd grown up in Chicago and spoke of how, as a west side lad, he'd rarely seen the suburbs. "I didn't know Chicagoland even existed, Brother."

"I'm still not sure it exists. Its ontological status seems uncertain to me."

"That's the college boy talking."

"Yeah, it is. It's a fancy way of saying that Chicagoland seems so weird to me sometimes that I wonder if it's real."

Abe went on, nonetheless, to act as though every strip mall, every exit, every boxy building—and even the Fox River between Elgin and Barrington—was quite real. I could have told him everything seemed tacky and ersatz to me. But I decided not to. It would have made for an interesting conversation, but I decided to let him talk and I would listen and monitor my own thoughts at the same time. I was also driving, so if you want to commend me for my multi-tasking I will take an overweight bow the next time I see you in the frozen food aisle at Wal-Mart.

I was thinking to myself that I hadn't become a cop for any of the usual reasons. I had no interest in finding the guilty and protecting the innocent. If you'd asked me about "public safety," I'd have said that was as important as the Marengo-Hampshire toll booth on Interstate 90: something you race through the transponder of so you can get onto the next topic or mile. Some people become police because it's a job. Other folks like the danger. I became a cop for none of those reasons.

I became one because I'm addicted to answers. When Professor Wilma Riddlehauer at Beloit College told me I was a budding professor I imagined myself for a while going about my business—my professional business—asking questions and answering them. I would ask questions and answer them for my students, and I would do the same in my learned articles. Some of my questions would be so silly they'd be profound, such as "Is Chicagoland real?" And then I'd proceed to answer the question by dismantling it: "What do we mean by real?" And after a while I saw it as a game, and while I liked the game, it wasn't for a west side of Beloit kid with a mild eating disorder from a blue collar family. It was too effete. It was too abstract: profound/silly questions and silly/profound answers.

But by then I'd gotten hooked on questions and answers and so I joined the police force. For a while I, skinnier then, worked in uniform (public safety: it was like manning a toll booth). But I knew I was quick and that I would eventually graduate into questions and answers. These are all questions and answers of fact, not of ideas. One reason I got drawn to Wittgenstein at Beloit College was because he had no patience for "Is Chicagoland real?" He would have said that if it weren't real, then you wouldn't be able to shop at one of its strip malls, and if you couldn't do that, then you couldn't buy yourself a discount watch, and if you couldn't do that, you couldn't tell the time, and if you couldn't do that.... But I also realized that I had little interest in good and bad. I just wanted the answers. I wasn't into the guilt and innocence thing.

I have a wee speck of right and wrong, and I thought my old partner Roger Webb was wrong to kill the husband of a woman he wanted for himself and to make it look like justifiable homicide and to play me, along with others, for a fool. That was wrong of Roger. But I was more excited about finding him out, even if I knew nobody wanted to listen to me (they still won't). I could still tell Dez. I'd found my answers.

That was the buzz of the thing.

Make me Mr. Question-&-Answer-Man; give me Dez as my unofficial partner; and let me become the awful wedded husband of Mary Webb, Roger's ex. Paradise would become, or so I thought, found again, though I'm not sure that it hasn't always been mislaid in my life.

How do you regain something you never had?

How many cars did I pass on that trip to Barrington? I have no memory of even having turned off on the exit to Margaret French Bryce's house, or was it a home? I can't recall whether Abe directed me or if I did it myself. This is scary. People should not reflect and drive at once. But I came out of my reverie of shallow self-examination as we pulled up to what can only be described as the most classical McMansion you'll ever want to see.

It had all the features of an old English manor house—the sort that lorded it over a baronial estate in the 1600s or so—but it was made of wood, not brick or stone. It had a plastic look, as though timber could somehow have been transformed into Legos and made a unit of residential construction. It was big and yet looked as though any wind over 30 mph would blow it down. It didn't seem well anchored. It had your three stories plus four front dormers. Mrs. Bryce had even put lightning rods on the roof for effect. Benjamin White himself, maybe, had come along to paint the house oatmeal-colored. It had no extended front porch, and only one front entrance. The door was a modest job of off-white trimmed in dark blue. It had a plywood look. It was though the owner had built this great and imposing domicile only, at the last moment, to skimp on costs and make everything else standard suburban. Abe and Elizabeth's front door north of Menard's looked more substantial than this one did.

Sergeant Woodruff and I weren't going into this part of the investigation ice-cold. We'd done some digital stalking and learned that Jonathan Bryce and Margaret Bryce were officially separated and had been for over a year. They had lived on the Gold Coast of Chicago, where Skip's tragically late brother had continued to dwell, while Marvelous Margaret had fled to Barrington where she'd built her somewhat bullying and surely tacky domicile just down the road from a new addition of mostly one-story split-levels, like Abe and Elizabeth's.

There was no butler. Abe and I couldn't even spot a footman, but we figured, later, that there must have been a live-in maid. How could there not be? Mrs. Bryce herself—the former Ms. French—answered the door. I was surprised that she had big hair—as though Dolly Parton had gone into flecks of gray—but her face was so unlined as give potent rise to suspicions of Botox. She would have been mid-50s.

And Skip was right: She had a long-faced equine look and was at least a few inches taller than the average woman is.

She sat us down in a living room as large as a small high school gym. Abe and I sat on a long modernist-looking orange divan supported by set-back curled aluminum legs. Mrs. Bryce plopped upon a low-slung chair that swung slightly when she placed herself upon it—a rocking chair effect. Everything seemed to be made of particle wood. Was Mrs. Bryce, for all her wealth, an IKEA nut? It wasn't hard to imagine her, cheerfully Midwestern, assembling everything between breaks of mint tea and ginger snaps. Just as I'd suspected, the whole interior had a fragile barn feel. This young manor house had not had a chance to settle down into impregnable form over a period of several hundred years.

And I'd bet it never will.

She talked like a decent, wholesome, optimistic Upper Midwestern woman who had, nevertheless, learned that there was far more in hell and earth than dreamt of in her former outlook on life. She was super-nice and hospitable; very solicitous of us as she offered us coffee or tea, iced or hot. She had a pleasant, chirpy way of talking that was at odds with her weary bitterness. It was though as Betty Crocker had turned into Gore Vidal. She even had some of Gore's sneering wit.

"I don't know what you gentlemen want to find out from me. Of course someone from your department tracked me down here and told me: Jon's been shot to death and left in front of a museum. I've not seen or spoken to Jonathan in over five months. I can't believe he got himself killed. How could he have done that? Why was he in Beloit, his hometown, when he'd not set foot there for years and years? I'm thinking that you people can tell me far more than I can tell you. I hope we can have a great visit on that."

"That's just the problem," said Abe. "We don't know any of those answers. You're going to have to help us."

"That's great, but I don't see how."

"Well, people we interview tell us that all the time," Abe went on. "Yet they help us. Something comes out, and it gets to be big later."

"Well, OK. That's great!"

"Let's start, Mrs. Bryce, with what sort of guy your late husband was."

"Canny. Shrewd. Opportunistic. Operator. Sorry to be so blunt. My parents taught me to say nothing if you can't be nice. But you said you wanted information, right?"

"Did you love him once?"

"Once I got swept up by him. I was a college student, and there was Skip, and he was a little earnest guy, awkward and timid, and I was sort of touched by his devotion to me. Then big brother came along, and this seemed to be the real deal. Do you know what I mean? He had a huge personality; very glib; flattering. Jon looked like he was on his way to Somewhere Important. Skip was happy if he'd not made any fielding errors in the big game against Lawrence. He was terrible with the bat and found fouling one off to be a victory. He was a mouse. Jonathan was the lion who roared. My father adored him."

"And didn't he work for your father?"

"You gentlemen have done at least a little homework. Yes, he did. My father had a string of shops he called 'The Exercise Store,' and it was a lucrative retail concept because you could go there and find everything you needed to find relative to your exercise regime. This was at the dawn of jogging, and he sold the shoes and the stopwatches and the running shots and shirts. He sold dumbbells. He didn't sell balls of any sort. Everything was related to self-exercise, not group exercise. Backers told him it wouldn't work. But it did. My father was an audacious gambler, so The Exercise Store had outlets mostly in the burbs from Elgin to

Waukegan and as far south, even, as Streator, though that was a fairly tiny shop. That's why my father liked Jonathan. He too was outsized and ambitious. I really think I fell in love with Jon because my father had fallen in love with him. Jonathan was always going on about 'why don't we do this?' or 'I've got an idea.' My father liked men with ideas. Skip, poor baby, had no ideas. And then Jon suggested to me, when I was about to graduate from Ripon, that if Skip did have an idea it was to fall in love with his best friend on the baseball team. So in Jon's view his little brother was a milquetoast and when he wsn't that he was a pervert waiting to happen. Look, I don't say that I'd have been happier with Skip. Skip probably is a worm. I don't know anything about him now. But Jonathan turned out to be a four-flusher deluxe. I wish I didn't have to say that. As I say, my mother always wanted me to be polite."

"I understand you two had a child," said Abe.

"We had a child, but it lived only a year. It was what I suppose you'd call a damaged child. It was born with a birth defect that killed it. I don't know why I'm saying *it*. *She* had a name, for my mother Lynn. Lynn—or little Lynn, as we called her—had a terrible gastrointestinal system that interfered with her ability to take and absorb nourishment. The doctors tried everything, but she just wasted away over time. That was over twenty years ago."

"Did that affect your marriage?"

"You're Mr. Dropsky, right? Yes, Sergeant, it did. And it did for a very simple reason: Because Jonathan showed that he wasn't about to invest in a losing proposition, and Lynn was a losing proposition. He took no interest. He took no interest in her or in what the doctors thought or in what my feelings were. It was about this time that the exercise ski machines came into popularity. My father was ill and ready to turn it over to Jonathan, who had this bright idea of filming commercials where somebody comes into The Exercise Store and tries out one of the ski machines and can barely coordinate himself or herself on it. But then there are a few more shots, and each time the initial customer gets better at exercising on these contraptions and in the last shot he or she is going a hundred miles an hour on it with strong, slim muscles. And the whole thing began, awkwardly, at The Exercise Store, so the idea was that when you entered the store you were this doofus but by the time you finished with the whole process or purchase and practice you were a world-class Nordic Tracker. These commercials were all the rage for a while. You may have seen one there in Beloit. It made us all a mint. It was Jon's idea. He even produced them."

"And when was this relative to the time of Lynn's losing battle?"

"It was at the same time. Lynn was struggling to live, and Jonathan was never there because he was busy making exercise commercials."

"And you were bummed? You were offended? You were hurt?"

"Our marriage never recovered, and after a while—once Jonathan started seeing other women down on Rush Street—I just decided there was no point. He was starting to look seedy and worn (too many drinks), and I've always prided myself on maintaining at least a wholesome appearance. Call me square. I know. We had a lot of money. I built this place and moved in. He stayed downtown. We agreed that divorce was too sticky and costly and that we would be separated and say as little to one another as possible. I'd married a brilliant but gaudy man. I was young. I'd given it my all. I had money. This place is far too big for me, but that's the whole point. I can explore rooms I don't need. I can take a holiday in my own monstrosity. I'll just finish off by telling you this: I can't really believe that somebody murdered my husband. But I'm not totally surprised. He would fawn over everybody, even the doorman. But he was a phony and a cold fish underneath. I can see how someone might come to hate him. He was no angel. I used to call him Mr. D.A.G. Mr. Devil in Angel's Garb. That's *DAG* for short."

"You used to call him that?"

"Yes."

"Did you do so to his face?"

"Never. But I'd mention it to my girlfriends. I think I told my mother about it once. She passed away last year."

"How did your girlfriends feel about Jon?"

"They didn't know him well, except to speak to on occasion when they were visiting me. They sympathized with me, though."

"Who else knew about this DAG business?"

"No one. It's more my own in-joke."

"Did anyone from the Beloit Police Department tell you about the museum where your husband's corpse was found shot to death?"

"They said a museum. That's all."

"Well, it was an Angel Museum," I said. "Someone else might have known about DAG. Did you mention it to anyone else at all?"

"I can't think I did."

"Where were you," said Abe, "between 5:30 and 7:30 PM on Sunday night?"

"I was here, watching Sixty Minutes or PBS or something."

"By yourself?"

"Yes. What's an Angel Museum anyhow?"

"A place where they leave devils in angelic powder blue suits," I said. "What was on Sixty Minutes Sunday night?"

9: Medieval Times

Abe drove on the way back to Beloit. He said: "Before we start talking angels, Brother Jeremy, I got to double-check with you on one thing about this case. What's going on with tracing the recent activities of the late Mr. Bryce?"

"Charlie's handling that part, or at least that's what I'm getting. In fact, I believe he told me he was going to supervise some of our fine colleagues to find out where Jonathan stayed in Beloit, if he stayed overnight anywhere, and where he might have been seen around town. Now it needs to be Charlie to get onto the Chicago cops and figure out what, if anything, Bryce did in Chicago to get him iced in Beloit. Forensics says that the murder occurred locally. Mr. Bryce was not transported as a corpse over any significant distance. His carass was too fresh for that."

"So the answer lies in Beloit or Barrington or Chicago."

"That would be my sense, too, Abe. I think we're wasting our time if you check into Charleston, South Carolina, or London."

"With winter coming I'd like to check into Charleston, South Carolina."

"It's a date. Now should we talk about angels?"

"If we must, and we must. I'm not looking forward to it, Brother Jer."

Abe sped up as we passed the Medieval Times Theme Park. I think this was his way of saying he *still* didn't want to talk about angels. Back in medieval tims they believed in angels.

'OK," I said. "So you and I both know the same things. Jon Bryce was found dead in front of the Angel Museum, and his alienated widow has said she used to call him a devil in angel's clothing."

"Garb."

"Garb. Right: D.A.G. Now we seem to be invited by somebody—don't ask me who—to put these things together. There are two questions, as I see it. Do we accept the invite and try to put these two things together? Or will we get off track if we try?"

"I can't see why a little assemblage here in the car will hurt anything, Brother Jeremy."

"Good point, Bro Abe. So: here we go. Margaret Bryce hates her husband so much that she has him bumped off and his corpse left in front of the Beloit Angel Museum. This is a cryptic sick joke: The Devil is left dead near a bunch of Angels."

"Had him bumped off is right. I can't see this lady carrying a Raven .25 unless it's got cream for winkles inside it."

"Agreed. So she has this devil of a hubby killed by someone else, who agrees to leave his body in front of the Angel Museum. This way there's a satisfying symbolism to her vengeance."

"Correct, unless she told somebody else about this D.A.G. nickname."

"Who else?"

"Here, Jer Bro, we get into trouble. She could have told anybody. She says she only mentioned it to her girlfriends, but let's just suppose that they told somebody who had a bad case of the hates for Brother Jonathan. Then the whole angel business becomes somebody *else's* symbolism."

"And, if you're right, we'll have a devil of a time (no pun) tracing who said what to whom about D.A.G. This is why this whole thing, if it comes out of Chicago, needs to be re-thought."

"I won't say re-thought," said Abe. "We—or Charlie and his section—would have to look into Chicago anyhow. But I can't see Charlie getting on the phone with Chicago cops and asking them to go door-to-door in Jonathan's apartment building asking his neighbors if they've ever heard him called a Devil in Angel's Clothing."

"Garb. Now you're getting it wrong."

"I sit behind the wheel corrected. But I'm right, right?"

"You are right. But we might be able to theorize our way out of this."

"Oh, no. Not one of your theories again."

"Yeah, most of the time they don't work out, I guess."

"I thought you were into this Sherlock fellow who said you shouldn't make theories before you got the facts."

"I am. But we'll never get these facts. We'll never find out who said what to whom about D.A.G. So we have to theorize in order to find the facts."

"You're losing me."

"Am I? I'm pretty lost myself. Ever heard of a guy named Occam?"

"Unless he was a hood in Champaign-Urbana, no."

"He was a philosopher in the Middle Ages."

"College boy stuff again. Shall I drive back to Medieval Times so we can have a talk with him as a consultant?"

"Great idea, but no, not yet. Anyhow, you're right. I did study him at Beloit College, and he said the simplest explanation that fits all data is the best. He didn't say it was always right. He said it was the best: the most likely. Of course sometimes the competition is pretty slim. That may be true in this case."

"So?"

"So you start not with the fact that Jonathan was left in front of the Angel Museum. You start with the fact that he was left in Beloit, Wisconsin. Then you go to Skip's inability to supply a solid alibi. Then you go to Margaret's D.A.G. And what do you get?"

"Whoa, Brother! She said she hadn't been in touch with old Skip in years."

"Maybe she was stating an inaccuracy."

"Are we talking conspiracy here?"

"We might be. But I admit this is pretty reckless stuff at this point. You're right, Abe. There's too much we don't know."

"But Charlie and Company will find out more, right?"

"I hope so. I don't want to spend the rest of this case thinking about the symbolism of angels."

"I go to church every Sunday, and I have yet to hear the word *angel*."

"Send a note to your pastor and ask him to keep it up."

10: Dialing Up the Hour of Demise

We got back to headquarters—or as Abe likes to call it, "hindquarters"—around mid-afternoon. It looked deserted. Only Rose and a few uniforms working on reports for the database were around. "Where's everybody?" asked Abe.

Rose said, "We've had a bunch of wrecks. A cement truck went into the ditch off Highway G/Martin Luther King. We had a big rain here while you guys were in Chicagoland. I guess people couldn't see through the deluge, so we've had some fender benders, too. Everybody's out writing tickets or yanking on a cement truck."

"You can't go into the ditch off Highway G. There aren't any. It's all level ground with the road. And why should all our uniforms be out on fender benders?"

"Well, Sergeant Dropsky, the ditches were a figure of speech, and I didn't say these were all minor fender benders. There can be major fender benders. And nowadays we tend to err on the side of caution with any auto accident. Pressure comes from insurance companies. You're behind the times, and you've never arrested my sister Susan."

"Half-sister. Not true. I detained her once for driving her wheelchair into the ditch off Highway G. Where's Baxter and what does he have out of Chicago on the late Mr. Jonathan Bryce?"

"He's contacted Chicago police and we're waiting to hear back. He's gone home for an hour," said Rose, frowning like a billowing storm cloud and looking big enough to be one. "No doubt he's processing a Moscow Mule about now."

"Are you saying that our chief of detectives is having sex with an animal?"

"No, Sergeant Woodruff, I am not. You too are behind the times. A Moscow Mule is Charlie's favorite new drink on the road to killing himself."

"And such a drink is?"

"Vodka and ginger beer, I think. Do I have to know everything for you guys? I thought you were the detectives. I'm just a humble receptionist."

"Who happens to run the force."

"If I run the force, how come I can't get my scheming, crippled roommate half-sister arrested?"

"Because we know that hating her gives you an aim in life."

We were about to leave early ourselves when Charlie, mulish or not, showed up, ramrod tall and straight and looking more like a stricken martyr than ever. How the man suffers, always admirably patient and annoyingly cryptic. Welcome to my life.

"You two need to get in here," he said, opening the door to his office. Charlie's late wife Gretchen, now dead these three years of head cancer, draped by a huge silver picture frame, smiled sweetly at us as though to illustrate the helplessness of us all against life's manifest injustice. For some reason I mused that it was unfair that Diana was dead while Prince Charles lived on. But this wasn't Charles. This was Charlie talking to us. He scowled at us and started chewing his syllables.

"I've got some big news on your case. First, forensics and the pathologist have dialed up the time of death. It wasn't late afternoon or early evening. It was closer to midnight. Don't ask me how they screwed up. I don't know. But I'll tell you this: they got it right because we have located the whereabouts of Mr. Jonathan Bryce here in River City. It didn't take more than some calling around. He was staying at the Beloit Inn and visited the bar there until closing time, which was 11 on Sunday night. He was alive until the doors closed. And get this: He also planned to spend the night there. It's all in the credit card data. Or have I said that already?"

"Wait one holy hell of a minute, Charlie. Are we to understand that Bryce never got to his room that night because he was dead?"

"We found his luggage in the room, and the bed was not turned down, Abe."

"Jesus Christ and General Jackson."

"Isn't that my line? And I assume the bartender or barmaid is our source of information here. So when Bryce left at around 11, what direction did he go in? Was there any memory on that?"

"As a matter of fact, Jeremy, that is one excellent question."

"No need to get sarcastic, Charlie."

"Life seems sarcastic these days, Jeremy. It isn't me. It's life. But yeah, Mr. Bryce tried to go through the back door of the bar and out onto that porch they have by the river. This was before the rain started, which was at around 3 A.M. Arthur the Barkeep told Bryce that the door was locked but if he wanted to see the river he could go around the hotel and that there was a nice walking trail back there all done up in the finest cement just for Mr. Bryce to stroll on."

"Arthur the Barkeep?"

"Arthur Simpson. Mr. Simpson to you, Jeremy."

"OK. So this was at 11, and he was killed maybe around midnight."

"Around midnight. And according to Mr. Barkeep the late Mr. Bryce was in the bar for about an hour fifteen minutes."

"So when he left the hotel bar he hadn't more than an hour to live. And what did Mr. Bryce do, according to Mr. Bartender Simpson?"

"He went out the front door. Simpson doesn't know what he did after that."

"But he well might have headed for the river trails."

"Looks that way to me."

"Anything else Mr. Simpson recalls?"

"Well, this is probably irrelevant, but yeah: He remembers Bryce's powder blue suit because there were two guys in the bar that night with light blue suits on."

"OK, and so he remembered the one because there were two, and this was unusual."

"Correct, Abe."

"All right, Charlie and Abe: this changes a lot. For one thing, we have to go back to Skip Bryce's alibi. It doesn't matter whether or not he can prove where he was early evening on Sunday because that's not when his brother was killed. So this whole thing about Columbus Circle is as big a wild goose chase for us as Skip says the trip to Janesville was for him."

"Not necessarily," said Abe. "Maybe Skip had been told that his brother was going to be shot earlier, if he had it hired."

"Now it's my turn, Brother, to say Jesus Christ and General Jackson. And, hey, what do you want to bet that Skip's going to say that he was already in beddy-bye by around 11 Sunday night, when his brother was drawing his last beautiful, powder blue breaths. And what do you want to bet that as a single man, long ago spurned by the future Mrs. Bryce who married his bro, he can't prove that he wasn't lurking outside the Beloit Inn waiting to shoot his brother to his eternal reward in Hell?"

"Yeah," said Charlie. "So?"

"So?"

"So where does this leave us?"

"Well, gentlemen—Sergeant Woodruff, Detective Baxter—I think it now becomes pretty important that we see whether or not Skip Bryce's trip to Janesville actually happened. So far we have no concrete proof that it did. As far as I know, the flyers in that neighborhood have produced zilch. I'm sure Charlie would have told us had it been otherwise. But even so, we have to find out whether or not Skip made that trip. I'd say that if he did, he's in the clear. He's not lying about anything. If I thought he wasn't lying about that, I'd be inclined to believe him if he says he was in the Land of Nod near Turtle Creek when his awful wedded brother was bulleted to death. We can eliminate Skip from our inquires, or almost can."

"I don't totally agree, Brother Jer. For starters: would his own brother come to Beloit and Skip not know about it?"

"Maybe Skip was to find out about it next day."

"There's that. I agree. But being in Janesville at 6 when his brother was killed at 11 doesn't eliminate him at all. And besides that, how are we going to verify Skip's cock-and-bull story about his fool's errand to Janesville?"

"How indeed, Brother Woodruff. How indeed? You tell me."

11: A Paradox, Not Too Red & Not Too Wet

While I was waiting for Abe to tell me how we would unpack Skip's alibi—and he never did tell me, and I couldn't tell him why it even mattered with the new time of death—I decided to go home. It was getting on 5. We had our new wrinkles in the case. We had new information. We had nothing out of Chicago. And Abe and I were so flummoxed by Baxter's new angle on time of death and the sighting of Jon in the bar that we didn't even mention to our immediate supervisor what we ourselves had learned about Jon's estranged wife's nickname for him and what, if anything, that had to do with the placement of the body.

New homes are brightly lit. They light up like shopping malls. When we went inside Merry Margaret's McMansion it was almost as though we were still out in the sun. My house is the polar opposite, by which I mean that if her house is at the equator, mine is closer to the North Pole. It's dark and unwelcoming. I've got no light fixtures in the ceilings, so I have to count on lamps. I should get the walls painted white and get some cheery yellow chairs and a fake ivory coffee table. If only Mary Webb were living here, she'd know what to do. She'd say, "Jeremy, darling, this place needs cheering up. You're living in a coffin here." Mary isn't here. Mary won't be here. In fact, I don't think Mary's ever been here, though her no-good husband Roger, my ex-partner, used to stop by for a chamomile cocktail (gin and herb tea) every now and again.

Dez scrambled downstairs. She said she could use one of those German-made snacks I get at Pet-Smart in Janesville, where the old Menard's used to be off the Interstate. These are meat sticks that you break into pieces. I call them her "Angelas" after Angela Merkel (don't forget to pronounce the *g* hard). Dez said she wouldn't mind at all if I gave her an Angela or two, and so I did.

We settled in to discuss our day. I could hear the whirr of the microwave as my Marie Callender chicken rigatoni evolved from frozen to hot. Dez munched while I told her about Charlie's new information and about Mrs. Bryce's D.A.G. She said she'd been touring the whole town looking for anything powder blue but hadn't spied a thing that color that wasn't plastic. Well, that told me, don't ask me how, that powder blue had something to do with this case. Powder blue might be the key to the whole thing. But I had no more idea of how than Dez had an idea about Wittgenstein.

Then Dez also told how she'd sneaked, once more, into the Angel Museum, but that she'd not seen any devils disguised as angels there. All the angels, she said, were on the up-and-up. Well, that told me that probably no one associated with the Angel Museum had had anything to do with this shooting. It wasn't an inside job, and Dez said, in effect, of course it wasn't an inside job, since the corpse was found outside the Angel Museum. It was an outside job.

This made me think that just maybe angels had nothing to do with this thing. Maybe it was all a matter of powder blue.

I asked Dez if she'd seen any powder blue angels at the Angel Museum. She said no. Well, there goes that theory.

She said she'd stopped in on Susan, Rose's wheelchair bound sister, who was at home in their battlefield apartment on the far north side off Prairie Avenue. What was Susan doing? Not much: fixing herself coffee, popping peanuts out of a jar, and reading her murder mystery set in Cleveland. For Susan, suggested Dez, mere existence gave her a purpose. She couldn't get around too well and seemed to have decreasing interest in doing so. The main thing was to be there when Rose got home. Susan knew that Rose hated her so much—there's no issue as contentious as a late parent's affections—that Susan had become, for Rose, not a person but a condition. So in Susan's eyes—or so Dez thought—keeping herself nourished with peanuts was sort of a way for the cancer to feed itself. And this is Rose's cancer we're talking about. Susan is Rose's malignancy.

I thought about how people fall out with each other. Take our victim Mr. Jonathan Bryce. He had fallen out with his brother. He had fallen out with his wife, whom he might have stolen from his brother. Susan and Rose had fallen out with one another. Roger and I had fallen out, though that was Roger's choice. Mary and I have never fallen *in* with each other, so that doesn't count.

But there was Abe and I. We were still friends. We had a good working relationship. There was just one problem: neither of us had a goddamned clue about how to solve this case. And one of the last things Abe had said to me today was, "Jeremy, Brother, even if Skip's Janesville alibi comes together it doesn't clear him of this, and if you think so, then that college boy logic of yours has failed you again."

Yeah, I had to admit it. Skip could have been looking for a sale in Janesville and still have been gunning down his brother several hours later. But if his alibi, which he no longer needed, was straight-on somehow—if he really was in Janesville looking for this crazy woman and her hubby— that suggested to me that he was an honest man; even a bumbling man; not a cold-blooded killer. But there was still the question of why Jonathan Bryce would have been in Beloit in the first place if he hadn't planned to see Skip. Still, is Skip—who can't even find his way to the right house in Janesville—the sort of guy who lures his brother to, let's say, just behind the Beloit Inn so that he can plug him?

I didn't care what Abe said. If Skip really did go to Janesville, then that was a sign he was innocent of all of it. It wasn't logical proof. But it was a sign, damn it.

Dez meowed for another snack. She jumped into my lap and started rubbing her face on mine. It was soft and cozy. She was rewarded with another Angela, or should I say *yet* another Angela. She said she couldn't help me with the Skip-in-Janesville business. Observation was her business. She had no degrees in sign-decoding.

I watched an old episode of *Game of Thrones*; two actually. I went to bed. I slept, perchance to dream. Check that. I *did* dream.

And I dreamt of powder blue angels. Dez said they didn't exist, not in Beloit. But this was a dream. Dreams are in this world, but they are also out of his world. This is what my old professor at Beloit, Wilma Riddlehauer, would call a paradox.

At some point during my slumber I saw that I was floating down Pleasant Street. It was unclear what was keeping me off the ground, and whatever power it was, it was erratic. At times I would seem to be coming down only to ascend in a nanosecond before my feet (which were bare) could touch the yellow line of the street. The college with its hill, and its red brick art museum perched thereon, were plainly on my right. The old Catholic Church that is now the Angel Museum was swiftly coming up on my left. I wanted to land so that I could investigate the area and willed myself down with no expectation that I had any influence over whatever was keeping me afloat. Yet I did come down. The walk in front of the Angel Museum was ice cold to my shoeless, sockless feet. I began to look down, studiously, for clues, but suddenly I felt a fiery leap in air temperature. I looked up and saw two angels, their wings black and their faces red, daring me to stick around. They said nothing, but soon it was clear that they were *un*welcoming me. They held long swords out of which fire came in intermittent but regular intervals, like the small blaze that comes from working oil derricks. Their swords had handles of sinister-looking diamonds set against a background of powder blue. I ran from them on chubby feet as fast I could, only be lifted again by the strong force of windy thrust that had carried me along, erratically, before. It whooshed like the force of air conquering the vacuum that nature famously abhors. I was whisked to a strange neighborhood. But the street sign had a familiar name: Columbus Circle. I saw all manner of houses from Hacienda bungalow to two story Tudor half-timber. I came upon a squat gray house with French doors, a dwelling redeemed by them and them only. I squinted to see the street address, but I could not read it. I was blown ever closer, yet the nearer I got, the more blurry the number became. Something scratched me. It felt dry and wet at once: another paradox. My eyes glared in terror.

Dez wanted another Angela. It was 4:37 A.M.

12: Sinner Jerry and Pastor Jimmy

I didn't sleep too much after that, but as a great advocate of trundling on despite all barriers I managed to waddle into hindquarters that morning and went straight to the computer. I was a fat man of enormous purpose and didn't even bother saying hello to Rose or asking her how much she despised Susan today. I did the usual thing with the mouse, and as soon as Abe came in, I told him we needed to take a car ride.

"Whoa, Brother! Are you arresting me or kidnapping me? Car ride to where?"

"Janesville."

"Yeah, OK. I love to travel, as you know, as J-ville is one of the garden spots. Seriously, Jeremy, what in the good Lord's Heaven are you up to? And it's too early for jokes."

"No jokes. It'll take us 25 minutes max to get there and if nothing pans out, 25 minutes max to get back. If Baxter asks, we can tell him that we were out looking for blood and heart tissue out behind the Beloit Inn. By the way, don't you think the rains washed most of that away after the hit on Jonathan?"

"I've thought of that, Brother Jer. And now you're calling it a 'hit' and that opens up a whole new can of fireflies and you want me to go to Janesville, to boot. Last I checked, we were Beloit cops."

"Trust me."

Abe did. He was intrigued. He decided to give me the edge in his by now considerable skepticism. He knew I wasn't nuts, just odd. He knew I had my own ways. He knew I was a good guy at heart, just lonely and a little overeducated. He knew I liked him. He knew I relied on his sanity and dependability and his insights. He knew I needed an honest partner. He knew he was one.

I drove, and for some reason Abe wasn't inclined to be chatty. I think he needed the trip time to be alone with his thoughts. He needed to double-check why he had agreed to be in the car with me on this errand, whatever it was. He knew that I wasn't going to tell him anything because I was also a smart-ass who liked to impress people with how smart I was; and yeah, it's true: I'd never quite accepted the fact that I was maybe a little overqualified for the job. I was a garbage spill, but Abe, good-hearted Abe, decided, at least on that sunny warm morning in September, to accept me as such, for a while anyhow.

There was another reason I didn't tell Abe any details that morning: because there was a reasonable chance that I had gotten everything wrong.

It had been about a year ago that Abe and I were driving back to the shop when we passed by Joyful Jerry's Used Car place and saw a couple of uniforms in serious negotiations.

It was obvious to Abe and me, a couple of seasoned observers, that this was some sort of mediation thing. The men in black and blue costumes are often asked to police the peace by getting people to shake hands and walk away. This was what was going on here.

One of the guys was an old pot-bellied fellow who was all stomach and no ass. His black trousers looked like a window drape because there were no buttocks to stop them from doing so. This man was at least 50% gut. "It's Pastor Jimmy," said Abe to me. "I know him."

Abe was driving, and slowing.

"Do you want to stop? This isn't our beef. I don't like to barge in on our uniformed colleagues."

"I want to stop," said Abe. "I know Pastor Jimmy, and Pastor Jimmy looks upset." He parked on Joyful Jerry's lot, right next to a fine looking used Buick Roadmaster.

We got out. I said, "Brother Abe, you got to give me a scorecard here: Joyful Jerry, Pastor Jimmy. Who are you, Awful Abe?"

But Abe wasn't for joking. He sped up his walk, that graceless shuffle that looked like he was barely moving his legs, and which belied his four-second 40 or five-second fifty or whatever he ran in high school. I ran a four-minute 60.

"Pastor Jim, what's the trouble?" said Abe to Preacher Gut Man. The latter looked about mid-50s. Gray hair with a big sprig of it stuck up like a sub's periscope.

"I'll tell you, Abe. I'm glad you're here. This sinner in front of me has cheated a member of our congregation."

Right away I found out one thing—that the sinner was none other than Joyful Jerry himself (a.k.a. Gerald Rathskeller, who lived in Pecatonica when he wasn't palming off used Oldses for profit). A bit later I learned that Pastor Jim was not Abe's pastor and wasn't really a pastor at all but a sort of lay preacher at one of the local churches. But Abe and Elizabeth were spiritual folks and knew a lot of other spiritual folks. Beloit just isn't that big. Either that, or the spiritual folks are not dense on the ground, so there's a small community of them.

No, I didn't wonder if they worshipped powder blue angels. Powder blue angels weren't in my purview back then.

"Now wait, Pastor Jimmy," said Abe, who by now had stepped in front of the two guys in uniforms, who seemed at once annoyed that they'd been replaced and relieved that somebody else had taken over. "What do you know about car deals?"

"I used to be a car dealer, Abe. And this sinner has given Sister Cora Calaboose a crummy deal. She told me. He bilked her on the trade-in. He threw in all sorts of phony pre-payment charges. I saw that on the bill. I'm down here to tell him to repent; to change his ways; to give Sister Cora a square deal."

"And," piped up one of the uniformed police, one Bobby Lehrmann, "that's when someone in the office here called us. Pastor Jimmy, as you call him, Sergeant, has been getting a little out of hand."

"Have you? Did you threaten Jerry here?"

"Yes! I threatened him with hell fire and damnation."

"In other words you raised your voice and started scaring the staff and other customers and started to frighten Joyful Jerry." This was me talking. I decided to put a more secular spin on this thing.

"That's exactly right, Mister," said Joyful Mr. Rathskeller, not so joyfully.

"OK," said Abe. "Now we got to settle this. The three of us, you (Pastor) and Jerry and I, are going to go into Jerry's office. We're going to close the door. We're going to pray over this. We're going to ask the Lord to guide us as to a peaceful resolution. We know the Lord does not like dishonesty, but we also know the good Lord does not like shouting down at the auto dealer. So we've got to stop thinking of ourselves and start thinking of the Lord and what the Lord wants because without the Lord we would not be here at all."

Gerald Rathskeller looked heavenward in disgust. But Abe is a man with a powerful physique and an attention-getting presence. He was on fire for the Lord and he was packing heat, too. Joyful Gerald saw a way out of this embarrassing fight, and Pastor Jimmy James couldn't say no to prayer. So off they went.

The rest of us waited, by which I mean the two uniformed cops and the two salesmen and the pert receptionist. We talked about what sort of winter we were expecting and whether or not the Packers would ever win a game without Aaron Rodgers. We were, let me tell you, into some really heavy stuff when the three of them—Abe, the smiling cadaver Jerry, and the Pastor Pot—emerged from the back office. Pastor Jimmy and Joyful Jerry thanked Abe profusely. The former got into his car sheepishly and drove away, but not before shaking hands with The Sinner. Abe said to me, "You and I and all constabulary may now exit the premises. Elvis can leave the building."

"What in Hell....?"

"What in *Heaven*, you mean, Sergeant Dropsky. Jerry will give Cora an extra three hundred cash for her trade-in and waive one third of the pre-payment charges. He'll still make out like a bandit. Pastor Jimmy will tell everyone what a fine man Joyful Jerry is and recommend that everyone buy a pre-owned Jeep from him. This is an even better deal for the Joyful One. God has spoken, and God has endorsed win-win and happy compromise. End of story."

"This is not the end of the story, Abe, not as long as enquiring minds, like mine, are still around. Who is this Pastor Jimmy and how do you know him?"

"Our churches sometimes worship together. Pastor Jimmy is what you call a lay supply pastor. He has no degrees or license, but he'll preach if you need somebody. He's not all there; looks like a bowling ball painted white with fiery eyes where the finger holes ought to be. He's retired now; forced to: been everything from funeral home driver to railroad router; says he sold cars once, too. Pastor Jimmy is a strange man, but prayer fixes him every time. And, oh, he loves the Lord."

That was when I took my first real measure of what a take-charge guy, what a very creative fellow, Abe could be. Abe had something I didn't: some folks call it emotional intelligence.

I still don't think Abe can talk to Dez. I at least have more feline intelligence than he does.

But while I was rendering us mobile in the Janesville direction, I thought back over the tale of Joyful Jerry and Pastor Jim, and I thought: "Abe thinks that I let him have his way then, so he's letting me have my way now."

Well, now that I look back on it, once this case had been solved, I think that was a silly idea on my part. Abe got in the car with me on our way to Janesville because he was as curious as anyone else to see what a fat sucker obsessed with an orange tabby and misunderstanding Wittgenstein the philosopher would come up with next. Abe was playing audience that morning. And he thought, "Why not? They aren't paying me enough to do otherwise."

13: Estelle's Universal Law

Well, I thought as we pulled up to our destination—my destination, I guess you'd have to call it—here goes. Abe and I gazed upon a house that my mother liked to call " whomp-a-jawed," which was her term for when things didn't fit together right. I think she might even apply that appellation to her own son. The house had a front, yes, but there was no door, and the facade was this skinny wing of the house, which was painted a sort of light puke green (shades, admittedly, of my own humble dwelling to the south). The "front" porch was screened-in, but it was on the side of the house, so your view on balmy summer days was of...a sliver of the ivory brick Cape Cod number next door. This seemed to be scenically attractive in the most minimal way. But where was the door? Well, it was on the *other* side of the house. After a little walking to and fro, Abe and I finally found it.

But on the door-less front of the house the address number was plain: 1552. Make that 1152 Columbus Circle. Yes, there is no 5512 Columbus Circle. Skip Bryce was quite right about that. But there is a 1552 Columbus Circle, and it was my humble opinion—or primitive guess—that 1552 Columbus Circle would become, for Skip, 5512 Credibility Avenue.

A man with a bulbous sort of face and a salt-and-pepper goatee opened the door to us. He wore a white t-shirt and wrinkled brown slacks. It was hot, especially for a September morning. The guy had a nasal and sort of Southern accent, though later I discovered it was southern Illinois. They talk a little twangy down there, far too close to Arkansas for a speech therapist's comfort.

"I'm Joe Cupps. Can I help you?"

"Yes, Mr. Cupps," I said, "you might be able to. We're from Beloit, with the police department. I'm Sergeant Dropsky, and this is Sergeant Woodruff." I could catch Abe gazing at us in wonder and trepidation. He had his "what the f" look. I knew it well.

"Well, we don't get to Beloit very much. But if you think I can help you, then we'll have to see about that." He seemed relaxed and droll, not defensive. That might be a promising start.

"I'm wondering, sir, if you live alone or with someone. Are you married?"

"Of course. I'm married to Estelle. She's not quite up yet. She sometimes sleeps in until ten. Why?"

"Has she been in touch with anyone in Beloit about life insurance?"

"Why, no. Well, look, I don't think so. Not that she's told me. But Estelle, well.... Anyhow, is this about some sort of insurance fraud?"

"Scam?" Now it was my turn to say "why, no."

"Well, if it isn't about a scam, then I'll have to ask her if she knows anything. I guess even if it was a scam, I'd have to ask her for you gentlemen to get the information you need. What's this about anyhow?" Suddenly he seemed a tad more taut.

"Mr. Cupps, we're checking out an alibi. That's all. You and your wife haven't done anything wrong." This was Abe talking. He'd tumbled to my theory and was riding it the way George Jones the country singer once got on his riding lawnmower and headed to the local liquor store.

"Oh, well, all right. Do you mind if I take a little time to get Estelle out of bed? Now, I've got to tell you men something. Estelle, well, she's a little peculiar. The docs don't quite know what it is yet, but her brain might be a little off. There might be something wrong up here (he tapped his skull). But they've also said it could just be some emotional thing, whatever that means. We've been married for over twenty years, Estelle and I have. I inherited enough money from my favorite uncle down in Carbondale; enough to retire on. I guess I was his favorite nephew, too. Well, I was his only nephew. He never had kids of his own. He never married, and he didn't like my dad all that much. Anyhow, we moved up here to Janesville because Estelle's sister lives here. We don't have any kids either, Estelle and me."

"Is Estelle from Carbondale, too?" This was me talking. I didn't want Abe to take over my project here on the off chance that it might actually amount to something. I was reasserting control!

"Born and bred. We've known each other from high school. Let me see if I can rouse her."

Mr. Cupps ambled into some back room. Abe and I later agreed that we'd imagined the inside of the house being as odd as the outside. We figured Mr. Cupps needed a GPS or something to get through the maze of rooms back there. We heard muffled voices. The female voice screeched in a high register. It was the sound of an alarm. The male voice was muted but sounded reassuring. It seemed that Mr. Cupps was trying to pacify Mrs. Cupps. We thought he was saying, "Now, Estelle, these policemen just want to ask you a few questions. They don't think you've done anything wrong."

This went on for the better part of ten minutes. Then the two of them emerged from the apparent maze—or was the maze in their brains—and by now Joe had put on a white dress shirt. It seemed, though, that Estelle had her own wrinkled trousers, though they were purple, not brown. She had a white blouse on, and over all this mélange of purple and white she had a sort of housecoat of many colors, all in various shapes of splotches. I thought of the red blots of blood on Jon Bryce's dead body, and made myself think that somehow this whole trip would contribute to the solution of his murder.

To this part of my theory, I would draw vigorous opposition. But that was later.

"Gentlemen, this is my wife Estelle."

Estelle was the proud if addled owner of an oval face with glazed blue eyes and a nose that Aspen could have used in winter. She was a brunette out of the bottle. There were flecks of gray where the dye had been remiss. She nodded with a blend of suspicion and de-animation. You could tell something was wrong. Yeah, she'd just gotten up, but you had the feeling that even after Estelle had been up for a while she still acted as though she'd just gotten up.

"Now," said Mr. Cupps, "why don't you gentlemen ask Estelle what you told me about?"

"All right. Did you call a Mr. Bryce in Beloit about getting a life insurance quote?" Abe again: he was taking over like this whole thing was his idea. Oh, well, I thought, let him: if it doesn't work out, then he owns some of it, too.

"No," said Estelle suddenly coming to life. "Well, what if I did?"

She had returned all at once from a long trip to the clouds. It was a miracle. Her face went from vacant to harsh. Her lips creased tight, and you could hardly tell her tongue was moving. There was a ventriloquist effect. She wasn't all there, but to the extent she was there it was a fierce there.

"I think, Love, these men just want to establish an alibi. Isn't that right?"

"It is right, Mr. Cupps. Well, if you wanted a life insurance quote, Mrs. Cupps, that's entirely your business. Did you ask Mr. Bryce to come to the house here?"

"Nothing wrong with that."

"No, there's nothing wrong with that. That's business. Now Mr. Bryce said you wanted him to come to the house here so that your husband could be present while he explained policies. But, Mr. Cupps, you weren't aware that Mr. Bryce was going to drop in?"

"I didn't know about this. If Estelle called him, why, then, she did call him. But he never came. I don't know a Mr. Bryce." Nor did he know, I'll bet, a "Gloria Warren."

"No," said Abe, "he didn't arrive. He was looking for 5512 Columbus Circle."

"Well, sir, we're not 5512. We're 1552. Why would he think we were at 5512?"

"I'm thinking, sir, that perhaps Estelle, I mean Mrs. Cupps, may have given him the wrong address."

"Estelle! Did you do that?"

"Men take their chances when women call them."

I took this statement as Estelle's Universal Law. I'm no doctor, but I thought that Estelle's problem wasn't neurological or emotional. She just had a personality afflicted by halitosis. I imagined that Joe was the functional one, while Estelle, unable to cope with everyday life, was his project. I further imagined that theirs was a happy marriage. Estelle was Joe's retirement aim in life, and Estelle was there, in all her sullen glory, to be aimed at.

"Why did you think we needed life insurance, Love?"

"Wasn't sure we did. Just thought we needed somebody to explain it to us."

"Well, Mrs. Cupps, were you planning on having Mr. Cupps here when Mr. Bryce arrived?"

"Can't recall. He never made it. Men."

"She doesn't really mean that, gentlemen. She's tired. You've gotten up too early, haven't you, Estelle?"

"And who's fault is that?"

"This is a delicate question, I guess, but does Mrs. Cupps sometimes get numbers mixed up?" This was Sergeant Woodruff again.

"Maybe the man wrote it down wrong."

"Yes," said Mr. Cupps. "Estelle is right. Maybe this Beloit fellow wrote it down wrong. You should ask him." This was the first time Mr. Cupps got a little snippy in his slow molasses-dripping way, and I couldn't help note that he had done so in defense of Estelle and I drew my own conclusions from that.

"Well, it doesn't matter. The important thing is that Mr. Bryce was called to come to this address. And, Mrs. Cupps, was this meeting to occur on Sunday afternoon?"

"Sunday afternoon."

"Well, that's all we need to know. We can be on our way. Oh, one more question: Mrs. Cupps, do you have a telephone credit card?"

"Is that against the law, too? What if I do?"

"All right," I said. "That's a good enough answer for now. I'll write it down in my report as an implied yes."

"Before you go, how did you find us if Bryce wrote down the wrong address?"

This was a logical question for Joe to ask, though I wanted to say, "You mean how did we find you if *Estelle* gave him the wrong address?" But Joe's question as stated deserved an answer. So I gave him one.

"I had a dream about angels with flaming swords and powder blue hilts."

Joe blinked. I think at that point he got thankful that there was somebody in the world even crazier than Estelle.

14: Oh, God!

I had never seen Chief of Detectives Charles A. Baxter look so crucified. He must have felt he had been hanged on a cross of blubber brain—mine, in fact.

"Now let me see if I can get this right again, Dropsky. You and Woodruff drove to Janesville—that's Janesville, Wisconsin 53545—to establish an alibi that is no longer relevant. Is that correct?"

"Yes," said Abe. "It seems so." He seemed to bow his head, as Ray Charles says in that blues song, in shame.

"No," I said shamelessly. "It is relevant. It's just not relevant as an alibi. I can't help it if forensics and pathology got the time of death wrong."

"But I told you they'd gotten the time of death wrong. If you hadn't know that, if Woodruff hadn't known it, then this trip north would have been understandable. But you both know—we all know—that Bryce was killed about five hours later. So if brother Skip was in Janesville earlier in the day, that does nothing for his alibi. He's still in the frame."

"Yeah, Charlie. And we knew that and yet we went to Janesville anyhow."

"That's what I can't understand: why you would waste taxpayers' money and the precious time of this department doing something that makes no sense at all."

"I agree. It's not an alibi. But it's important anyhow."

"From what you tell me, this Estelle and Joe are quite the couple. Why did she call Bryce for life insurance in the first place?"

When Charlie asked this question, I thought: "Now who's going off on an irrelevant tangent?" Well, if it kept his fury away from us a little while, I'd play along.

"I don't rightly know, Charlie. Estelle didn't seem to be the strictly logical type. [I wondered if Charlie still thought *I* was the strictly logical type.] She might have thought she and Joe needed some security. She might have been trying to make Joe jealous by inviting another man to the house. She might have just been bored. You know, even people out of their gourds suffer from ennui."

"Suffer from what? There goes College Boy Jeremy again. Well, don't think you're going to get me off the track. I've got to know whether you and Woodruff here have taken leave of your senses."

Abe was a stand-up guy. "I went along on this trip because I trust my partner, Charlie. I still do."

"But why? If you and he are going to look to establish alibis that aren't relevant to the time frame, then I can't trust either one of you."

"I keep telling you, Charlie. It isn't an alibi. It's a piece of the puzzle, and it tends to exonerate Skip. Now do I say he's out of the frame? No. Even somebody as knuckle-headed as I am knows that he could have been looking for the wrong address at 6 and murdered his brother at 11. But we thought he was stringing us along with a fake alibi, and it turns out he wasn't. This trip to J-ville really happened. It went down just as Skip said it did."

"But that does not eliminate him from the frame, damn it!"

"No, but it almost does."

"You are losing me, Jeremy. You are really, really, really losing me."

"Well, OK, let me see if I can find you again, Charlie."

"How? Hell, go ahead."

"Well, if Skip knew that he'd killed his brother at 11, he'd have never bothered to give us an alibi, which he couldn't prove, for 6. He'd have just said that he was home at 6 watching *Sixty Minutes*."

"But Brother Jeremy, we *asked* him about 6." My logic was even too much for Abe.

"Yeah, but he was so naïve that he tried to sell us on a story that he knew he couldn't verify. He was totally not clever about it. He would have known that lack of proof would make us suspicious. But he went ahead anyhow, because in fact the story *was* true. People who tell cock-and-bull stories that are true tend to be innocent. They have a trusting quality. I know a story about a kid who said he saw President Lyndon Johnson at a graveyard. His parents whipped him for lying. Turns out he did see Johnson at the graveyard. This was in Texas one time. A guy I knew at police academy told me. Skip's that kid who said he saw

Johnson. The kid knew his parents wouldn't believe him, but he told it anyhow, because it was true. This establishes Skip as an ingenuous fellow, the sort that doesn't kill his brother in the darkness."

"Did you say 'ingenuous?'"

"Yes, I did."

"And this is when I get to say that I don't know what that means and also that I don't want to know. This nice kid Skip, as you call him, could have had an argument with this brother behind the Beloit Inn and plugged him."

"We have no gun traceable to him."

"Not yet, and he might have hired the work done."

"I don't think so, Charlie. You can call this intuition if you want. But I think there's a sort of 'way of life' logic about finding out Skip's Janesville story was true. And this 'way of life' logic tends to clear him. I agree he's not out of the frame. But to my mind he's almost out of it. Once upon a time I was hep on him staying in it. Now I'm not."

"Where do you get this 'way of life logic' business, Jeremy?"

"It's from Wittgenstein, Abe."

"Oh, God."

"I agree with Abe's oh, God. By the way, Jeremy, how'd you get onto this correct address anyhow?"

"It sort of came to me in a dream, with angels with flaming swords and powder blue hilts."

"Dreams. This Wittgenstein guy."

"I know," I said. "Oh, God."

Charlie's laptop whistled. He'd installed some sort of referee sound on it to indicate a new email. He must have thought he needed a break from me, however short. He wheeled his chair over to the screen. He squinted, he smiled, and he said: "Well, Jeremy and Abe, maybe all is forgiven. Come over here and read this!"

15: A Stolen Raven

Charlie Baxter had gotten what is called "vital information" from one of the many foreign cops he'd cultivated in Illinois, and he ordered Abe and me to investigate it right away. But "right away" got interpreted by Sergeant Woodruff and myself as "right after lunch." I headed out to a sandwich shop on the big highway towards Milwaukee, ordered my 25 kinds of meat and 19 types of veggies between a sour dough roll and fished out my cell phone. I didn't think I'd get Professor Riddlehauer at Beloit College. I was wrong. She was in.

I needed reassurance.

So I told her, in hypothetical terms, about my reasoning where Mr. Skip Bryce's alibi was concerned, and about my attribution of my logic to Wittgenstein, whereupon she told me I was quite wrong.

"Jeremy, look. It's good to hear from you. Come back to us. Audit my class. But hey, you're a little confused here. There may be, in theory, places where people who concoct absurd alibis that turn out to be true can't possibly be murderers. Wittgenstein thought there were all sorts of communities with all sorts of beliefs. But that's not the grammar of the cops, as you should well know. You guys don't deal in folk psychology about people. You deal in physics."

"Physics?"

"Physics. You deal on the assumption that a person can't be in two places at once. So if your hypothetical suspect can't prove that he was somewhere else at the time of the killing, then he's still a suspect."

"But the guy's alibi for the earlier part of the day turned out to be true. And I just think that somebody who was that bumbling and that naïve can't be a murderer."

"Well," said Wilma. "That's your psychological reading of his character."

"But it has nothing to do with Wittgenstein?"

"It has nothing to do with Wittgenstein. I fear, Jeremy, you've just pulled out old Ludwig in order to justify your conclusion. You've misread Wittgenstein, but you usually read him well."

"OK. Well, that's something anyhow." Wilma Riddlehauer was tall and willowy. Her body parts didn't seem to fit, like the Cupps's house. One hip seemed higher than the other, as though to say that no body mattered a damn next to a big brain that sat magnificently atop the torso. She wore her granny glasses around her neck when they weren't perched keenly on her nose. It was as though those glasses were like night goggles that could see, through dark knotty fog, what no one else could. She was cheery and formidable, Wilma was; a philosopher as good in philosophy as Dez was in catnip and observation. And now she'd told me I'd gotten Wittgenstein wrong. Well, all right. I had. But that didn't mean I was wrong about Skip Bryce, whom I thought was as innocent as the sweetest and littlest angel in the Angel Museum. My gut told me he was. And I have a big gut.

I had to eat my super sized sandwich fast since I'd spent precious minutes on the phone with Professor Riddlehauer and couldn't talk with food in my mouth, not even on the phone. I was due to meet Abe back at hindquarters at 1:15 and got there at 1:20. Rose said Abe was waiting for me in the conference room (a.k.a. Predicament Room) and that she hoped we were gathering to figure out how to arrest her stepsister.

"You're late, Brother. Let's not let old Charlie catch us getting behind."

"Sorry, Abe. I had to make a phone call. I have to phone now in order to learn that I've gotten stuff wrong."

"What?"

"Never mind. So do we have anything new on this Jake Abernathy?"

"I think Charlie's getting too excited about this. So let's try to state it clearly. A neighbor of Margaret Bryce's in Barrington came to a Barrington cop and gave him a tip: that Marge was banging her handyman and that his name was Jake Abernathy. Now we don't know how this neighbor knew his name was Jake Abernathy, but that's not too hard to imagine. The houses aren't that far away from each other, Mr. Abernathy works outside, and Margaret's pile backs onto the back yards of the lesser folks in the area. So it

114

wouldn't be hard for a neighbor to strike up a conversation with Jake Abernathy and have Jake tell this neighbor that his name just happens to be....Jake Abernathy. Make that Jacob Abernathy, by the way."

"Yeah," I said, "and it wouldn't be hard to figure that said neighbor would notice that Mrs. Marge was pretty friendly with Jake Abernathy. They've had all summer to observe them." I imagined that if I lived there, Dez would have long ago reported to me that Jake and Margaret were smooching between the tomatoes and the lilies.

"Correct, Brother Jeremy. And then there would be the little item of Jake Abernathy's car and how it was parked overnight at Margaret's."

"Brilliant. Hadn't thought of that detail."

"Well, Sergeant Dropsky, sir, that's because you haven't read the full report, which came in a little while ago. I have read the full report, between 1:15 and 1:20."

"Yeah, I was late. Sorry again. So we have some solid reasons to think that Margaret was having it on with Mr. Abernathy, and the Barrington cops have checked and Abernathy has a record as long as Plastic Man's arm, and this has gotten Charlie juiced, so that he's even thinking about forgiving me for having a dream and figuring out Skip's non-alibi alibi."

"Right. But now we've got to consider just what kind of record Jake Abernathy has."

"Don't tell me. He's never been arrested for cold-blooded murder. He's never been indicted for it. He's never been convicted of it. OK. But has he any sort of arrest record for violent crimes?"

"He has. He's not quite a career criminal, but he's close."

"Let me give you, Sergeant Woodruff, my definition of a career criminal. Between his 18th and 42nd birthdays lay 24 years. If he's been in jail for 13 of those years he's a career criminal."

"OK. Well, our Mr. Abernathy has missed, but only by a couple of years. He's been inside a lot."

"For?"

"Bar fights, where he got a little carried away and battered solid citizenry. He held up a dental office—you heard that right—at the point of a gun. He's done his share of shoplifting. He's filched some hubcaps and once stole a vehicle. He's quite versatile."

"He's never shot anybody? Why did he hold up a dental office—to steal the gold they use to fix the molars? Was the dentist the first cousin who used to taunt him as a kid?"

"Don't know. But they caught him for that and sent him up for eighteen months. There's no indication of whether or not the judge snickered."

"How much did he get?"

"Less than 400 bucks. I'm surprised it's that much. Most people don't pay cash for getting the holes in their teeth covered up."

"The man's a nincompoop. He's not the Napoleon of crime. We only have him pegged for using a gun once, and he didn't fire it. Any record on his gun ownership? This man's not likely to register his pieces."

"Ah, Sergeant Dropsky. Now I get to surprise you. No, you're right. No guns are registered to Mr. Jacob Buell Abernathy of Crystal Lake, Illinois. But: thanks to the magic of cross-referencing data technology we have learned, while you were making your phone call and having lunch, that Mr. Abernathy has a brother, one Jay Abernathy of nearby Woodstock, Illinois; and Mr. Jay A. does have a gun registered in his name, AND said weapon has been reported by the owner as stolen."

"And it's a Raven .25."

"Jeremy, you are a genius."

"No, I can just anticipate a good story. So: now let me continue the story. Skip Bryce and Margaret Bryce, having a mutual enmity against the scurrilous and amoral Jonathan Bryce, conspire to have Margaret entice Mr. Abernathy to kill Jonathan. But first they have to find an untraceable gun—one that has no link to Jake. Jake figures the easiest way to get such an instrument of destruction is to steal it from his brother. Jake does not realize that with today's computer cross-checking we can find such a link. They didn't teach him that in the pen. Neither do Skip and Margaret know this. They have now all fallen afoul of digital magic, and they will soon enough be joining Jake in the Big

House. Fortunately, however, he's been there before and can give them pointers. Jake has never fired a gun in anger before, as far as we know. But he'll do anything for a rich lady like Margie, who is fifteen years older. We are going to wrap this up in just a few days, possibly fewer. How am I doing?"

"Brother Jeremy, that is one mighty fine and righteous story. Do you believe it?"

"No, but we have to check it out. How do we do that?"

"By checking it out?"

"That's a mighty fine and righteous suggestion, Brother Abe."

16: A Stroll Through Downtown River City

Later that afternoon Abe and I met with Baxter to plan our next move. Charlie called Barrington again to talk to the officer who had gotten the tip about Margaret and Jake. The Barrington source said she'd gone over to the neighborhood to discuss the matter discretely with other neighbors, who confirmed that there was likely hanky-panky inside the McMansion. So this wasn't just one neighbor trying to dish dirt on another. In fact, said the Barrington cop, no one in the neighborhood seemed to dislike Margaret. They even thought it was a little amusing that she was seeing the handyman in the altogether. They didn't know about Jake's record of course. But while they thought banging the gardener was funny, they all seemed sure—and the Barrington fuzz talked to five of them—that it was happening.

"So let's say," said Charlie, "that the affair is real, and we know that the gun theft is real, and we know it was a Raven. Of course I'll have to get Woodstock police to interview Jake's brother about the stolen piece. But I don't want to do that yet. We have a record it was stolen, and only three months back. We need to find out if Jake could have taken it. Did he visit his brother around that time? Does bro even suspect Jake of the theft? But if we talk to the brother right now, or send Woodstock cops to do it, then we risk tipping off Jake. We know the gun was taken. We know a Raven was used to kill Jon Bryce. We know that Margaret didn't like Jon. We know that she, or think we know that she, is seeing Jake in the raw. There are a lot of links there, men...a lot of links."

"So what are you saying, Charlie," said Abe. "Are you telling Sergeant Dropsky and me that you think we need to talk to Jake and Meg before Woodstock re-interviews the brother? Suppose the brother says there's no way Jake could have filched the Raven?"

"Then we have some Grade A egg on our faces. But even if the dear bro does try to clear Jake, that doesn't mean Jake didn't take the piece. No. I say we surprise these two with a sit-down as soon as possible. Don't take a chance of tipping them off. Don't let them work together to get their stories straight. Drop in on them in Barrington. Take them down to headquarters there. Interrogate them separately. Shock and awe: that's my idea."

"Yeah, Charlie, I agree with that as far as it goes. But no matter how much shock and awe we may think we have, these two are going to say predictable things. Jake is going to deny that he stole the Raven. He'll get a lawyer to point out that we have no proof. This lawyer will also say that Jake has no history of gun violence. As for Margaret, I don't think she'll deny that she's banging Jake, but I don't think she'll admit it either, and she too will get a lawyer, and she'll say, with his urging, that it's none of our business whether or not she's keen on the man who removes the brush." That was my little speech. I didn't want Charlie to think he was going to solve the case with a surprise interview.

"Right, Jeremy. I get that. But we'll let them know we'll be talking with them again, and with the surprise effect they might let something slip. It's not a short shot. It's a Hail Mary. But I think it's worth a try. We'll do some more investigating, and Jake will have to supply an alibi, and we'll check it and if it isn't a good one we'll be seeing him again. He'll know that. This first bite at the apple is just to ruffle their feathers."

I thought Charlie might be mixing his metaphors a little bit here, but that's just ex-college boy talking.

I wasn't crazy about this tactic of Charlie's. It seemed to reek of load, fire, aim. But did I say "reek?" Now who's mixing metaphors? Bad strategies don't reek, do they? Only turds, or old tunas, reek. Yet the more I thought of Charlie's approach, the better I liked it. We couldn't really start the investigation of the Dynamic Duo of Barrington McMansion until we'd talked to them directly. We had to try to surprise them. We had to take their testimony, even if they lied, as an initial foray into evidence. So I was in. Charlie was a good cop, even if he didn't understand Wittgenstein. But then maybe I didn't understand him either.

While Charlie worked the phones to get our trip to Barrington set up with the cops down there, I told Abe I needed to drive home to get something. Luckily for me, he didn't ask what it was, since I didn't really need to go home for anything other than to speak with Dez.

She wasn't there, but when I went out back to call her, she presented herself. I told her hard-g Angelas were waiting inside for her if she happened to be interested, and she said she was. She hopped onto the kitchen table, and I pulled a cold cup of Taster's Choice out of the fridge. I like iced instant. I told Dez about our progress, or regress, on the case. I sometimes thought she was more interested in feasting than in listening, but I long ago learned that Dez has her own methods.

I started to envision Dez as a parallel investigator again, but this time I didn't send her out to check the Angel Museum. She'd already reported that she'd sniffed or spied no blood on any of the figurines, and that re-convinced me that the murder of Jonathan Bryce, though his remains were found in front of the Angel Museum, was not an interior project, by which I mean that no employee of the museum had anything to do with it. Dez had pretty much persuaded me of that with her various forays into the bloodless museum.

But now I sensed that Dez, having found nothing at the museum other than a few ceramic cherubim, now turned south and headed towards downtown. Where was she going? Dez looked at me with those green distant eyes of hers and raised her paw to clean her mouth. She was ever dainty after meals. I looked at her, brushed her face with the back of my chubby hand, and knew: She had stopped into the bar at the Beloit Inn. She had hopped up on one of the stools and ordered a Catnip Cocktail; call it a gin and nip if you must. I thanked Dez, gave her a few more sticks of hard-g meat, and excused myself. If she wanted out again, there was the cat door.

I drove back to hindquarters and visited Abe's cubicle. I told him I was back, and he said that seemed obvious, and I told him I was taking a walk.

"Taking a walk? You? Are you all right, Brother?"

"Fine. I just need some fresh air."

"Do you know it's ninety in the shade out there—hot for September? Well, sure you do. But I guess you'll stay out of the shade, right?"

"Something like that."

Abe was right of course. It was fifteen degrees above normal for mid-September, and I'm not a small boy and I sweated through my cheap suit. I waddled on nonetheless. I passed by the backs of the businesses on State Street and gazed upon doors marked "Bushel and Peck" and "Bagels n' More." I then took a left onto State Street itself and looked upon the latest edition of a small space on the east side of the street. Everything, it seems, had been there, but mostly restaurants of various sorts—from general diners to specialty Italian to faux French. I took a right onto Grand and couldn't help recalling the businesses there during my childhood, especially Drekmeier's Drugstore, where I read Super Boy comic books under the forgiving eye of the pharmacists, who knew I wasn't going to buy one. There's a sports bar in that space now. Finally, I veered left onto Pleasant and soon enough found myself, two pounds lighter due to sweat, at the Beloit Inn Potable Palace. I asked the world-weary lady with dishwater blonde bangs behind the bar if Mr. Arthur Simpson were round and about and if she'd be so kind, if he were, to fetch him. I told her I was a cop but that this was boringly routine business. I expected her to say that this was his day off or that he didn't start until 3 in the morning or something. I hadn't called ahead, so I wouldn't have been surprised if she told me he wasn't available. And while I told her this was just boring stuff, the truth was more complex: I'd taken this little hegira because I *was* bored. I found a mine vein, for she said Mr. Simpson was in the kitchen and that she would get him for me. Later I learned that he had minded bar the night Jon was there because he was filling in for the regular person. He was a sort of manager, and needed to be there a lot. That's why he was around during my unannounced drop-in.

Mr. Arthur Simpson was a young man. I wondered how someone with acne scars and a voice that gyrated between alto and basso could manage anyone. He was skinny and stooped, deferential but slightly annoyed. I apologized for barging in and told him I was just following up on an aspect of the Jonathan Bryce business.

"I've given a statement and signed it."

"I know, and it was helpful. You placed our victim in a way that was a big assist to us."

"Have you solved this?"

"We're making progress. Anyhow, I know you remembered Bryce's powder blue suit because there was somebody else in here with one on. So let's suppose there was just one powder blue suit in the place that night. Would you have remembered just the one?"

"What? Oh, I see. Well, maybe not. I don't really get into suit colors, and we do have a lot of guys in this place, from out of town, who wear suits. So no, if there hadn't been the two blue suits I probably wouldn't have remembered a blue suit at all. What was unusual was that there were two, both soft light blue."

"OK. Now this question you've not been asked. Were these two suited guys sitting close to each other?"

"Not at all. One was at the bar, and I think your fellow was sitting at a table closer to the back doors there. He wanted to go through them down to the river when we closed."

"Right. But the doors were locked then. Now you've also answered my next question, but I'm going to ask it once more. How many other customers were here at the same time?"

"As I said, five or six."

"And were any of them wearing suits?"

"I don't think so, but I can't remember. What difference does it make?"

"I don't know. Did you know any of these other customers?"

"I didn't know them, but then I'm not the regular barkeep."

"Were there any women?"

"I think so, yeah. I think there was a couple, but I can't remember much about them."

"Was the woman, say, about 50, maybe a young looking fifty with, like, a long face?"

"No. I can tell you that much. She was young, much younger than that. Like I say, there were five or six others besides the guys in the suits. I didn't know them, except, well, yeah, there was this guy in a pony tail. I may have seen him around here a few times. Think he could be local, but got no idea of his name or anything else about him. I think I just remember him because we don't get that many pony tails in here."

"OK, right. It's not 1968 any more. We may have to talk with you again when we develop some further leads. At some point we may have to run the credit card payments that night to see if we can locate anybody else in here who remembers anything. We aren't there yet."

"All right. I just don't think I can help any more."

"You never know. Thanks for your time."

I, dripping, trudged back to the station, and on my way into the refuge of central air, I met Gladys Earl the forensics guru of the department. She is a tiny person, and I've always thought that was altogether fitting and proper since she mostly dealt with microscopic evidence. But today she seemed, in my presence, to be shrinking before my eyes. The reason: she was apologetic.

"I've said this to nearly all the major players, Jeremy, but I've not gotten around to you. I'm really sorry about the snafu re: time of death. The path said '11' and somebody misheard and copied it down as '7.' The victim died between eleven and midnight. I know you and Abe went on some sort of unnecessary errand trying to establish somebody's alibi for 7 or so."

"Between 5:30 and 7, actually; and it wasn't totally unnecessary." My brilliant deduction about 1552 Columbus Circle had been deemed irrelevant, but I had my pride. Besides, Gladys would never know, so I decided to bluff and imply that the trip to Janesville had been a major step in the investigation.

"Well, I'm glad it wasn't unnecessary after all, Jeremy, though I'm not sure I see how it couldn't have been."

"Trust me, Gladys."

"I will, Jeremy." And with that she almost skipped back towards her office. I guess she was glad to get the last apology over.

So onward and upward would we go to the Barrington Encounter with Lady Bryce and her Lover. But something told me the key to the whole thing was right here in Beloit. Something kept nagging at me: that Dez had not visited that Beloit Inn bar for nothing.

17: Brothers

You don't just drive down to Barrington and interview a couple of suspects. There's the tiny matter of logistics, so it took our Barrington colleagues in the constabulary a day or so to set everything up. They had to locate Mr. Abernathy and have a pretty good idea of where he'd be at 9 in the morning when the pick-up was made. We'd have our little chat with him first. He'd be detained as a person of interest in the homicide of Mr. Jonathan Bryce of Chicago in Beloit, Wisconsin. He could refuse to go with them to the Barrington station, but they almost never do and "unlawful arrest" complaints generally get dismissed. A career scoundrel like Jake Abernathy would know that. So we decided we'd get there by 8:45 that morning, and by now we're talking Friday, five days after the body had been found among the angels. I picked Abe up out in the Turtle Creek burbs at 7:15 that morning.

On the way down I-90 Abe decided he wanted to talk about Skip Bryce again. I was afraid of that. Skip was a mighty tender topic of conversation for me. I'd started out insisting that we couldn't lose sight of him as suspect #1 and was now claiming his innocence based on a misreading of Wittgenstein and a non-alibi alibi that could only work if we repealed the laws of physics. I was sure Skip had nothing to do with this, but of course Abe wasn't. And he wanted to let me know just in case I'd forgotten.

"You know, Brother Jer, Skip could still be in on this."

"I know, Abe. I know. He could be. He just isn't."

"I wouldn't give up on the possibility of a conspiracy. I can see that Mrs. Bryce got hold of Skip and said, 'You know, Skip. We've both been scammed by this scumbag, and I've got just the man to put him out of our misery.'"

"This could have happened, Abe. It didn't. Would something that happened that many years back really fuel homicidal revenge? Only on TV."

"But for Ms. Margaret it wasn't many years back. It was only several months back."

"Granted. But for Skip it would have to be many years back. Are you trying to say that he and Marge decided that their years of wedded bliss had been prevented by lying Jonathan, and that they got together, the two of them, to put old Jon on ice? If that's your scenario, then how does Jake fit in?"

"Jake," said Abe, "could be the fall guy. He does the crime and pays the time, while Margaret and Skip finally live happily ever after."

"I can't see a still attractive and regal woman like Margaret falling, after all these years, for a beady-eyed runt like Skip. Now I'll admit he's a solid, hard-working, earnest, middle-class little runt. But he's still a runt. You can send a squirrel out to dig holes in the ground where other squirrels might live. But he's still a squirrel. Skip's a runt."

This was mean. I'm not so attractive myself—a walking whale.

"Anyhow," I continued, hoping to recoup my dignity in Abe's presence, "we'll try to find out if Jake's been a fall guy for anybody, or if he's about to become one."

"Fine enough, Brother," said Abe. "I still say we can't let Skip skip away."

The Barrington cops weren't precisely happy to see us. They were doing us a favor. But after they spent a little time with Abe, at least, they softened. Abe could make you feel good about life. They said they'd have our man with us by 9:15 A.M. at the latest. It was 9:13 when we entered the interview room. What must Jake Abernathy have thought of us—me an overweight slob with a Glock bulging behind a faded tan Goodwill coat and Abe dressed like he'd come out of a bandbox and shaking hands with Jake in that "mighty-glad-to-know-you" mode that Abe should have patented. This was also Abe's signal to me. He was going to play Good Cop today. I began.

"Mr. Abernathy. I'm Sergeant Jeremy Dropsky and this is Sergeant Abe Woodruff. We're from the Beloit, Wisconsin, Police Department, and we want to question you about the unlawful death of Mr. Jonathan Bryce late last Sunday evening. You are not under arrest. You can leave this interview at any time. You can ask for and get an attorney. This is not a Miranda warning because you're not under arrest. The only word of caution I can give you is that what you say here is being recorded and might be used later as evidence; and that what you say or don't say here may prompt further inquiry and interviews. Are we straight?"

Jake Abernathy was a grease ball out of Central Casting. He had a seedy, worn look, beneath which lurked a kind of lewd energy. He scowled at us from the brow to the chin of his long skinny face. But you could see right away that when he smiled somebody might think he was handsome in some derring-do way. He was the sort of guy that seemed to liberate sheltered women into all sorts of misadventures. He had a lavish black mustache. He had not shaved in a couple of days. He was dressed in work clothes. Barrngton had picked him up at a room he was renting, for rest, I guess, between bouts with the former Margaret French. I had to think: Margaret seemed a bit old and mature and upper middle class to be finding kicks in a hackneyed cat's ass like this guy.

"Beloit," said Jake. "Isn't that some little town over near Rockford?" Jake grinned with more than a particle of contempt. He knew the first move was his: He didn't know anything about Beloit because of course he'd never been there.

"We're a little bigger than small town," said Abe. "But you got the location right."

"Ever owned a gun, Mr. Abernathy?" Jake looked my way. Now, I'm sure he thought, I'll have to take my measure of the fat one.

"Not that I recall."

"Let me help your memory. Have you ever owned a Raven .25?"

"Not that I recall."

"Not that you recall. Well, sir, we'll have to take that as less than a flat no, so right there you're asking us to investigate further."

"OK, then. No, I've never owned a Raven .25."

"Have you ever seen or handled one?"

"Not that I can recall."

"Again, we take that as less than a total denial, so we'll be looking into that angle and will want to question you further no doubt."

"Again. OK. No, I've never handled a Raven .25."

"Well, you do seem to have no trouble calling the gun by its right caliber and brand, even though you've only heard it a few times. But we'll put that down to a good memory. Still, Mr. Abernathy, there's something about the way 'Raven .25' rolls off your lips that tells me you have more than a nodding acquaintance with the weapon."

For the first time, Jake blanched. The big guy was pretty sharp. I really think at that point he wondered about asking for a legal aid lawyer, but then decided against it so as not to turn up our suspicions higher than they already were.

"Well, Sergeant. I'm good at remembering things. That's all. No, I've never had anything to do with this, this type of gun."

"Does anyone you know own 'this, this type of gun?'"

"Who?"

"Please answer the question."

"I don't know anybody that does."

"Do you have a brother?"

"Do I?"

"Do you?"

"Yeah, We don't talk much. We sort of went to separate rodeos, you know."

"Does he live in Illinois here?"

"Woodstock."

"Does he own a Raven .25?"

"You'd have to ask him."

"Did you and your brother ever go hunting together as kids?"

"All the time."

"Did you use bow and arrow?"

"Of course not."

"Did you use guns?"

"Yeah."

"Did you and your brother ever talk guns?"

At this point Jake gave us a plainly panicked look, the sort that said, "I don't know what you guys know, or think you know, and that's really bothering me." At the same time, though, a guy like Jake doesn't trust cops, and sometimes imagines that they'll set him up as an ex-con. So this man is shaking inside, but that doesn't mean he's guilty.

Of course I would never let him know this complex mélange of thoughts. I was the prosecutor here. Make that persecutor.

"Yeah, we did sometimes as kids. So what?"

"Well, I'm just wondering why, after this rich and uplifting family history of shooting innocent deer, you and your bro would suddenly go into radio black out on the subject of guns."

Abe inserted himself with his million-dollar smile. He gave Jake every piano key he could find inside his merciful Christian mouth. Jake looked relieved. "I believe, Brother Jake, that your own sibling is Brother Jay. Is that right?"

"Yeah. Jay."

"And how often do you see Brother Jay? He's not far off, so I assume you two get together every now and then."

"Uh, not too often. Jay's a respectable guy. I'm a jailbird. Well, I was."

"When, Brother Jake, was the last time you saw Brother Jay?"

"Maybe, oh, back in the spring. I needed some money."

"And did Brother Jay, Brother Jake, give it to you? Lend it to you?" I thought Abe was walking a tight line between sarcasm and relatedness, and I could see that Jake was confused about that. It was one of Abe's techniques.

"Yeah."

"Good for Brother Jay. I wish I had a bro that nice. And where did you and your Brother Jay meet?"

"At his place in Woodstock."

"Is Brother Jay lawfully wed?"

"To Marjorie. Why? She doesn't like me. I thought this was about Beloit."

"All in good time, Brother." This was me talking. I decided to let Mr. Abernathy know that I too could get into this rich evangelical moment that my partner had begun.

"So was Marge there when you visited Jay?" Me again.

"Nah. Jay knows she hates me. She's ashamed of me."

"Do you think she fears you? You've been inside a lot."

"Probably, yeah."

"So where did you and Jay sit when you visited him at home? Maybe in the living room?"

"In his office. He sells real estate from home."

"Did he give you cash?"

"Yeah, he did. I thought this was about Beloit."

"Oh, we'll get to Beloit, Mr. Abernathy. Brother Jake. Don't you fret. So I'll bet Jay had to leave you for a while to get the cash. He doesn't leave cash lying around his real estate office. He had to make a quick trip to the bank, and before you ask, we know the bank is almost walking distance from Jay's house on Nugent Street. And this took maybe twenty minutes for Jay to fetch the cash and come back with it. He wouldn't write you a check because Marjorie would find out about it and disapprove. And you are left sitting in his office, and that's exactly where guys like to keep their guns: in their offices. A gun in an office makes you feel powerfully *official*. So if there's a gun in that office—and you and Jay have this lavish history with guns— you could have taken it. You might even have a good idea of where he kept it, seeing as how you know your beloved bro so well. And guess what kind of gun Jay had?"

"I don't know. I don't *know*!"

"He had this, this, uh, this type of weapon. What do we call it?"

"Raven .25?"

"Brother Abe, what a grand memory Brother Jake has about the type of gun that Brother Jay owned! And that's because Brother Jake stole this magnificent little piece from Brother Jay!"

"No!"

"And now we get to the location of Brother Jake's dreams: we get to Beloit, Wisconsin, that little town near Rockford, where recently a dead body was found shot to death by this, this, uh weapon of that type."

"A Raven?"

"A Raven! How smoothly off the tongue comes that expression from someone who has told us, Brother Abe, that he knew very little about guns and 'couldn't recall' whether he'd ever even handled one. Why, Brother Jake here, he can barely spell the word 'gun.' But he can quite easily articulate those magic words 'Raven .25.'"

Jake fell silent. He looked down. He looked back up with fury in those eyes, glassed over with dirty sleaze balls. "You guys are always trying to pin stuff on guys like me who've been inside. You can never let us go straight. I don't have a thing to do with anybody dead in Beloit. Never even been there."

"Never even been there! Did you hear that, Sergeant Woodruff? Next thing you know, I'm going to mention the Beloit Inn Bar, called Belwah, and after that, after just one mention, Jake here is going to remember that word 'Belwah' and he's going to repeat it with authority—all this from a man who says he's never been to Beloit, Wisconsin, where, I'll bet, he paid cash for everything."

Abe time: "When, Brother Jake, you say you're trying to go straight, what do you mean? What you been up to lately by way of legit business?"

"I'm a handyman and gardener."

"How'd you learn gardening?"

"I have a knack for growing stuff. You can ask my brother. When we were kids I had the green thumb."

"And I'll bet he had the better gun finger. Anyhow, do you have a regular customer or customers?"

"Yes. Mrs. Bryce."

"Hmmmmmmm.....," said Abe. "And I believe the man killed in our fair little town of Beloit was named Jonathan Bryce. Do you think they're related or is this just a coincidence?"

"What? Oh, OK. I see where this is going."

"And where is it going, Jake?"

"You think because I work for Margie that I'd kill her husband. My God!"

"Margie? Don't you call her Mrs. Bryce?"

"Well, she's a friendly lady. Classy, too."

"That's what everybody tells us, Jake: that Mrs. Bryce is a mighty friendly lady. And I've also heard that Ravens are extremely friendly little guns."

"How about angels, Brother Jacob. Do you know anything about angels?"

"What?"

"Angels."

"No."

"What about D.A.G.?" I said it instead of spelling it out.

"Dog?"

"D-A-G: it means Devil in Angels' Garb."

"No."

"You seemed so sure, Mr. Abernathy. The question didn't seem to surprise you at all. Why is that?"

18: The One-Syllable Queen of Tupperware

There was a fifteen-minute break between our chat with Jake and our visit with Margaret. Of course we made sure that the two of them met in the hall as Jake was on the departure level. This would presumably shake whatever zoo they were living in. We told Jake we'd be seeing him again, and he said next time we'd be seeing him and his lawyer.

During the intermission between Jake and Margaret I called Baxter, as promised. I gave him a short summation on Jake and asked him if there was any progress on what scene-of-crime operatives had found on the river trails behind the Angel Museum. Charlie was sure that Jon had been shot there and moved several yards to be left in front of the Angel Museum. In other words Jonathan Bryce began his last moments by the turbid flow of the Rock River and ended them mere feet away from Oprah's Angels. I supposed that Charlie, too, thought the location of the Angel Museum was code for something, if it was only somebody's personal code. Charlie Baxter thought Jon had been shot on the trails because, according to Art the Bartender, he had wanted to walk back there shortly after 11 P.M. I wondered if this assumption was warranted. Charlie evidently thought Jon had been plugged on the trails and moved near the

Angels but that a gully washer had erased all forensic proof of such an event.

"No, Jeremy. Scene of Crime has gone over those trails pretty good and found nothing. There was a gusher later that night, and I just think all blood and body traces were washed out."

"But absence of evidence doesn't mean evidence of absence."

"What? Dropsky, sometimes you talk totally nonsense. Just absolute rot."

"Well, whatever I talk, I need to close in on Margaret. She's waiting with her attorney for Abe and me to make our grand entrance."

I ended the call.

Margaret Bryce had taken a while to dress up for this event. Somebody at the Barrington Cop Shop had tipped her off about the scheduled happening, enough time for her to get her attorney and to become a clothes horse to go along with her equine visage. She wore a gray pants suit with a high collar. Everything up to the neck, and even a little beyond, looked masculine and efficient. Her light brown pageboy was impeccably coiffed. She smiled at us—the hostess with the mostess—as though to welcome us to a Tupperware party. She had this elongated face and a mouth too big for it. This aperture she quickly turned down as though, suddenly feeling the gravity of the situation, she had converted a thumbs-up into one going in the diametrically opposite way. The shift was remarkable. I wondered if the smiley greeting weren't a ruse she'd used before.

Her attorney introduced himself as Jim Stillinger. He was a big man, maybe mid-40s. He had a wrestler's build on its way to muscle tone loss. He couldn't button his blue suit coat and so kept it open at his great big torso. He looked a little like a menacing flasher. He spoke first and made it clear, for the record, that his client, Mrs. Jonathan Bryce, was here voluntarily.

Abe and I didn't want to quibble with this. We gave her the same little spiel, about rights and subject matter, that we'd given Jake, and were careful to add that this was not a Miranda because she wasn't under arrest and could leave whenever she wanted to. We assumed Jim would depart with her.

"D.A.G."

"Yes?"

"You remember D.A.G., don't you, Mrs. Bryce?"

"Yes." It was clear she'd been primed by Mr. Stillinger to hew to the monosyllables.

"And that stands for Devil in Angel's Garb?"

"Yes."

"And it was the nickname you gave to your estranged husband Jonathan?"

"Yes."

"And what was the tone of that nickname?"

"I don't follow you." This was followed by a pseudo-apologetic smile.

"Well, you seem to want to stick to yes and no, Mrs. Bryce. So I'll try to make it easier for you that way. Was the tone of the nickname bitter?"

"I guess so."

"I'll put that down as a yes."

"Wait a moment, Sergeant," said Jim Stillinger, heaving up off his chair a little bit as though to display what was left of his Killer Karl Kox world wrestling cred. "She didn't say yes. She said she supposed so." This was a remark just built perfectly for Abe and me to ignore.

"Were you angry at your estranged husband?"

"I suppose so."

"Well, he was estranged, so I guess that makes sense. What is your relationship with your employee Jacob Abernathy? Is it only professional, or do you have a personal friendship as well?"

"Both."

"And is your personal friendship one that has included sexual relations?"

"Don't' answer that, Margaret. She declines to answer."

"No need to take the Fifth. This isn't that kind of interview. We need to hear from Mrs. Bryce. Do you decline to answer?"

"Yes."

"All right. Let the record show that Sergeant Jeremy Dropsky concludes that if Mrs. Bryce were not having, or had never had, a sexual relationship with Jacob Abernathy she would have not declined to answer the question. Let the record show that Sergeant Abe Woodruff is of the same opinion if he so assents. Do you so assent, Sergeant?"

"Yes," said Abe. "I can do the one-syllable answers, too."

"And let the record also reflect," said Jim Stillinger, "that Mrs. Bryce declines to answer because it is none of the business of the Beloit, Wisconsin, Police Department."

"The Beloit, Wisconsin, Police Department is investigating the murder of Mrs. Bryce's estranged husband," said Abe. "And we were hoping that Mrs. Bryce would help us solve the murder."

"Well, let's move on. I want to help Mrs. Bryce stick to her short answers. So let me ask her this: Did you know a lot, a little, or nothing about Mr. Abernathy's background?"

"A little."

"Did that little include knowledge that he had spent nearly half of his adult life behind bars for various crimes?"

"Yes."

"Were you aware that Mr. Abernathy once served time for a violent assault?"

"No."

"Did you know that Mr. Abernathy has a brother?"

"No."

"Have you had any curiosity as to how your late husband met his death?"

"Yes."

"Does that curiosity extend to the sort of weapon used?"

"Not really."

"That's three syllables. Congratulations. Did you ever talk about lethal weapons with Mr. Jacob Abernathy?"

"Of course not."

"Three syllables again. We've got ourselves some upward progress here. Have you ever suspected Mr. Jacob Abernathy's brother of murdering your estranged husband?"

"What?"

"Did you ever suspect—or do you now suspect—that your estranged husband was murdered by Mr. Abernathy's brother, who lives, by the way, not too terribly far from Barrington?"

"What kind of trick question is that?" Jim Stillinger was ready to give me the chokehold.

"I believe the question is plain. Will Mrs. Bryce answer it or will she declined to do so?"

"No."

"Is that no I won't answer or is that no, I never suspected Mr. Abernathy's brother of murdering my estranged husband?"

"I never suspected."

"Six! Six syllables." The Tupperware greeting had long vanished from the face of Mrs. Jonathan Bryce. Her outsize lipsticked mouth puckered in fury. "O.K. Good. We've got that straight. Let me add that if it is true that Mrs. Bryce never knew that Mr. Abernathy had a brother, then it would be logical to expect that she would never suspect this brother, of whom she says she knew nothing, of murder. This all seems quite consistent, and I know, Mr. Stillinger, that you will find that good news for your client."

"Can we get on with this? Margaret and I didn't come here for logic-chopping."

"No, you wouldn't have." I was always a smart-ass, and fat smart-asses like me are especially there for despising. "Well, let me sum up so far, and you can tell us, Mrs. Bryce, if what I say is accurate. You decline to say whether or not you've had sex with your gardener. You've no interest in the details of your estranged husband's death. You were aware, though not totally, that Mr. Abernathy, said gardener, has been quite the jailbird (career criminal the sociologists call it). You were not aware that Mr. Abernathy has a nearby brother and never suspected him of murdering Jonathan Bryce in Beloit, Wisconsin, last Sunday night or early Monday morning. Oh, and one other thing: You have not yet offered an alibi for where you were at the approximate time of the homicide. Is that all accurate?"

"Be careful, Margaret."

"Yes," she said.

"Where *were* you on Sunday night between the hours of 11 P.M. and 1 A.M.?"

"Asleep here in Barrington in my own home."

"OK. Good. Let the record show that this is the first time we have *officially* asked about an alibi. Can you prove it?"

"I was alone."

"Well, of course you'd need to get to Beloit, Wisconsin, before you could fire any triggers. So what was on, say, PBS earlier this past Sunday night?"

"I don't watch PBS."

"What were you doing between 9 and 11 Sunday night, Mrs. Bryce?" This was Abe with his change-of-pace pitch. Now it was he offering the Tupperware smile.

"Reading."

"And," said Abe, "your fingerprints are on the book, but we can't time fingerprints, so we'll need to take your word for it. That's fine for now."

"All right. I've summarized what Mrs. Bryce has told us, and she has said that I'm factual about that. She gave us all the royal yes. So now let me also sum up some facts in evidence. Mrs. Bryce called her alienated hubby a devil in angel's garb. She has *supposed* that this was a moniker expressed in anger. He was found murdered in front not of a devil's museum but an angel's museum. He was shot with a particular type of gun (aren't they all), and this particular type of gun belonged to Mr. Jacob Abernathy's brother. This is the same Mr. Jacob Abernathy with whom Mrs. Bryce declines to say whether or not she's had sexual congress. Have I covered everything, Sergeant Woodruff?"

"You have, Sergeant Dropsky. But I also have another question for Mrs. Bryce. Did you, or do you, have any nicknames for Mr. Abernathy, such as 'you handsome devil you?' That would be as an acronym YHDY—hard to pronounce."

"This is way over the line," said Stillinger. "I guess they don't train cops well in Beloit, Wisconsin. We're out of here, Margaret."

"Let the record show that Mrs. Jonathan Bryce, whose husband was murdered in Beloit, Wisconsin, home of ill-trained cops, declined to answer any further questions." And with that smarmy declaration from Yours Truly, the overweight cat lover and pseudo-student of Wittgenstein, Mrs. Bryce and Mr. Stillinger rose in self-dramatic turmoil and rushed to the door. It sure seemed like a retreat to me.

Just before they got out the door, Abe did a facial number that landed somewhere between a grimace and a smile. He said, loudly, "And to think that Mr. Abernathy was so much more forthcoming with us!"

Well, what had we gotten done? Abe and I would have a long trip back to Beloit to discuss that difficult question. And thanks to a truck accident and the usual welter of I-90 construction we had over two hours to figure out the answer, if any.

19: The Distinct Possibility of Physics

As Abe and I made our overlong trip back to the shores of the Rock River (you can throw in Turtle Creek as a bonus), I suddenly found myself filling up with defensive, civic pride. How dare that smart-ass suburban lawyer—that Killer Karl Kox wanna-be wrestler—make fun of Beloit! That's my hometown we're discussing, buddy. I thought of our college, our sunken home designed by a student of Frank Lloyd Wright, our once world-famous explorer Roy Chapman Andrews. And I thought Abe and I had done our tag-team job pretty well on both Abernathy and Mrs. Bryce.

The question was: where had that gotten us?

Abe said, "We did what we could, Brother, and we did it well. But it isn't going to be nearly enough unless we get some evidence. This is what we don't have in this case: real evidence. We got no confession. We got no specific ballistics match. We got no eyewitnesses."

"But we do have a smartphone photo of Mr. Abernathy for presentation to Arthur Bartender."

"Yeah, we do. And I've checked. I took it pretty well. It's sharp. It's clear. If Abernathy was at Belwah Bar that night, last Sunday night, then Mr. Simpson should recognize him. If he does, we're in business. In fact, I don't know why we shouldn't bring Abernathy to Beloit for a little line-up. Might make him pee in his pants anyhow."

"I don't know if that would pass procedural muster, Abe, with what we got so far. But tell me two things."

"Start with number 1, Sergeant Dropsky."

"Will do. First, then; number 1: Do you think they did it?"

"Seems likely. Too many coincidences: angel, gun, estranged wife, new slime ball lover."

"All right. So you think the locale of the corpse, the late Mr. Bryce, in front of a museum dedicated to ceramic and marble angels, is significant."

"Yeah."

"OK. Number 2: What did we achieve today?"

"Other than showing we're a pretty good team? Well, we might have set up a little division in the ranks. One of them might flip."

"Which one?"

"I'm thinking she will. She can always say that she didn't put him up to it; that he did it on his own because he loved her; that she's just a good suburban lady who got mixed up with the wrong cat's ass."

"Yeah, but he's the one who's been inside. He knows what that's like. Don't you think he might try to make a deal to limit his future habitat as a guest of the government?"

"He might. But you know, Jeremy, he's enough of a career criminal to know that he can't avoid too much time. He's the trigger man. Any judge is going to see that this guy started with petty stuff and has now gotten his Ph.D. in first-degree murder with a deadly weapon. He can keep from going up for life, but he can't do much better than that."

"I agree, Brother Abe. Which one do we want to get off the streets more?"

"Now you're getting all philosophical on me, Jeremy. I don't like her. I think she's a schemer, and I don't like the fact that she lives in a McMansion and I just like in a Quarter Pounder with Cheese in Beloit, Wisconsin. But I got to say *him*: He's moving up in the ranks of violent bad guys, and he needs to go away for a good while."

"Well, you've said a lot, Abe. I wasn't sure how you'd answer. But I agree with it all. I'm not sure whether you've convinced me or I was in concurrence all along. But I do think they did it; I think she'll cooperate if we can find some more pressure and some more evidence; and that above all he needs to go on holiday to Waupun. We've got to get onto Woodstock. They need to talk with Jay Abernathy and see what he has to say about his stolen gun. I don't think *we* need to talk to him, not yet. Agreed?"

"Agreed. I don't think there's a rush, but after we get back to Beloit we need to do that. Clear it with Charlie, first, of course, but then do it, though probably on his advised schedule. Let Baxter make the call if he wants; or maybe he'd rather email. What do you think of that referee's whistle on his computer?"

"I think he put it on there because he senses time's up."

"What?"

"Well, when a referee whistles he's stopping play. He's saying that time's up. Charlie thinks the Great Ref in the Sky is going to whistle him dead pretty soon. He looks terrible. He's drinking too much. He's grieving. He's installed that whistle thing so he can get used to the fact."

"Jesus Christ and General Jackson, Jeremy! Do you really believe that?"

"No."

"Good man."

We shut up for a while. Then Abe said, "You know, even when you get out of town just a little bit, everything looks different. Look at Belvidere over there. I'll bet even their street people look different from ours."

"What about their telephone poles?"

"Them, too."

"Well, we need to get out of town more often, Abe. We need more crooks to chase down in places like DeKalb and Orfordville. We need to become telephone pole tourists."

"I'm an Oregon, Wisconsin man myself."

The construction and accident that turned our trip back to Beloit into a cross-country hegira nonetheless had a limited effect, so finally we pulled up into headquarters on the Illinois border. Charlie was insufferably around and asked us what took us so long. Abe said he wasn't in the mood to explain, but that we had a good excuse, and Charlie accepted that and looked slightly apologetic. I changed the subject at once and brought up Woodstock. He said he'd get on it before he left and agreed that Jay Abernathy needed to be interviewed and a report relayed to us. He didn't think we needed to talk with him, not yet. He wanted to know, too, of course, what we thought we'd managed to get done in Barrington. Abe and I, always the fine tag-team, did a little duet of talking points, all of which consisting of what Abe and I had decided on the way back home.

"Yeah," said Charlie at last. "I think you're right. We got no good evidence right now unless Mr. Simpson positively identifies Mr. Abernathy as having enjoyed a few Moscow Mules in the bar last Sunday night. We'll talk to Simpson soon and show him the pic. But maybe you've scared the Missus into giving us a true confessions call."

"A Moscow Mule is a drink, Abe, of ginger beer and something else—Red Bull, I think."

"Thanks, Brother Jer. That's very helpful."

"Are you mocking my drink choice, Dropsky? "

"I am not, Charlie."

"Well, I don't think we're very far along, but I think you two have pushed us an inch or two at least. Let's call it a day, and I'll call Woodstock. Tomorrow's Saturday, but I'll show Simpson the photo of Abernathy at some point in the next 24 hours."

I was starving for one of Marie's deep dish Parmesan chicken numbers, even if it did take ten eternally long minutes in the microwave, and I wanted to see Dez so I could go over everything with her. But I decided otherwise. I acquired a bag of Cheetos from the convenience store in South Beloit and rang Wilma Riddlehauer on my phone. By now we're looking at past 5:30 on a Friday. But she liked to stay late in her office over in Morse-Ingersoll Hall. It's a red brick job, built in the 1930s, with an odd shape, sort of like the Cupps's labyrinth house in Janesville. It took me a while as a student to figure out how the building was structured until I realized that it didn't make any difference which door you entered. You'd eventually end up in the same place. Between the two wings of the building—which is really just one wing—there's a tunnel, west of which is the classroom side of campus, while leading east is the residential side. You go ten yards in either direction and end up in a new world, one based on brains and the other based on bods.

Wilma hung out in the middle of this architectural melee. She answered on first ring and gladly accepted my offer of a late afternoon coffee down on Grand Avenue. "Coffee on Grand would be grand, Jeremy. I'm always happy to hear from the local constabulary, and this will give me a chance to urge your return, yet once again, to our fair college."

Within fifteen minutes Wilma was putting her erudite rimless glasses on her nose and looking across a latte at me. I with my waddle and she with her slightly angular gait removed ourselves to a table near the back door and started our chat in low-decibel voices, though not a conspiratorial whisper. I've always sworn that she listens with those glasses and not with her ears. I think there's some high-powered First Alert system embedded into the those spectacles, and it goes off in her brain whenever she hears something smart, interesting, or wrong. I could supply all three. I think that's why she liked me. I was like the sightless hog who sometimes found an acorn.

I swore her to secrecy, used aliases and misleading Illinois locations for the whole story, and laid it all out for her in detail. And then I popped my question.

"So what we've got here is coincidence, and we think it's meaningful coincidence—that the museum and the weapon and angelic nickname all add up to meaning just one thing: These are the people who did the crime. And yet, and I'm only telling you and my cat this, I'm not sure they did do the crime. How can I not be *sure* with all these coincidences?"

"Well, I don't know how much I can help, Jeremy. But I'd start by asking you: How common is this particular type of gun? If it's really common, then lots of other people could have used it."

"It's not super-common. But yeah, it's common."

"Well, that helps a little. If there were only 20 in the world, then your theory of coincidence would be stronger. And then there's the nickname about devils and angels. Now we know the popularity of 'wolf in sheep's clothing,' but what about 'devil in angel's clothing, or garb?'"

"I don't know. Is that a popular saying, too?"

"Well, let's put it this way, Jeremy, and I say this as a professor of logic trying to help out a bright ex-student. We do know that 'wolf in sheep's clothing' is popular. So suppose your victim had been found outside a Wolf's Museum—let's say, a museum devoted to types of wolves? What then?"

"Well, since we know that 'wolf in sheep's clothing' is so common, a corpse found in front of a Wolf Museum—even if that corpse had once been called by his hostile wife a 'wolf in sheep's clothing'—might not mean very much. I mean, it's such a popular cliché."

"I would agree, Jeremy."

"So I guess I need to consider whether 'devil in angel's clothing' is as popular and common as 'sheep in wolf's clothing.'"

"Right. Now we do know that the idea of devils versus angels is an old and popular one. Satan was a fallen angel."

"OK. So let's sum up, Professor, so far. The gun is common and the saying is common. So it's not like the wife called the husband a Dweeb-Ball, and he ends up dead in front of a Dweeb-Ball Museum. I'm suggesting that Dweeb-Ball, for instance, would be far less common than wolves and sheep and angels and devils."

"This is why I want you to finish your degree, Jeremy."

"Thanks, Professor. That means a lot. I probably won't. But thank you for the encouragement. Would Wittgenstein have anything to say about this? I tried to use his work to defend a non-alibi alibi and got nowhere, except with my cat, and you said I was wrong, too. But what about with this?" I think this question came from my not-yet-expired wish to become a college teacher instead of a cop— something I'll never have the innards to pursue.

"I doubt it, Jeremy. But here's one comment I would make from Wittgenstein's point of view. You're familiar with Wittgenstein's idea of atomic propositions, right?"

"Right."

"And Wittgenstein thought that atomic propositions painted a picture of reality, such as 'The present wrapped in white with a red ribbon is in the southeast corner of the room.' And he once thought that was all language could really be relied on to do: paint pictures of facts, or what he called 'everything that is the case.' Right?"

"Yeah, I follow. So?"

"So in physics atom 1 has nothing to do with atom 2. They just co-exist. They don't connect, And so the fact that the present is in the southeast corner of the living room has no bearing on whether, in the same house, the stove is in the northwest corner of the kitchen. So you've got one of two possibilities here, Jeremy. Either you're dealing in some sort of meaningful narrative, where all this stuff about guns and angels and nicknames matches up to tell a sinister story of murder; or you've just got physics, where the gun and the angel museum have no more to do with one another than do the locations of the present in the living room and the stove in the kitchen, or where atom 1 has no bearing on atom 2."

"Those are my choices? Narrative of physics?"

"It would seem so."

"My colleagues are into narrative, and so am I. But I can't shake the possibility, in my instincts maybe, that this whole thing is just physics: meaningless coincidence."

"Yes, it's just a coincidence that the present with the red ribbon and the gas-burning stove are in the same house. By the way, how'd you do in physics?"

"I got a C in it in high school."

I thanked Professor Riddlehauer, paid for her coffee, and pointed the pokey blue Mazda to the west side for a date with Marie Callender and Dez.

20: Cham & Gin

The latte with Professor Wilma hadn't done it for me, so I was more than eager to tuck into the deep dish Parmesan chicken pie that the microwave would conjure up for me in ten minutes' time. I'd suddenly decided ten minutes wasn't all that long after all. I always have a little trouble tearing the box open. It's cold, and I have fat fingers. Dez joined me within five minutes of my arrival. She heard the speed-challenged Mazda in the drive. But she'll never scamper in right away. She always withholds her presence for a short time, whether to express her displeasure with my absence or simply to let me know that she's not been idle during my time away and had to finish up a few tasks before she entered by the cat door.

I usually have water with my Marie Pies, but decided that a little iced Chamomile tea after dinner would be a unique delight on this starry Friday night in late summer. I fished out the carton, extracted several bags, and put on the kettle. So it was a race between the microwave and the kettle. The latter won, and I poured the boiling water over the bags into a pot. It would cool, and the resulting brew would be transferred to the fridge in short order. In due course I was able to enjoy the Parmesan chick—I fixed Dez a complementary can of grain-free meow mélange—and life seemed pacific enough. I couldn't stop thinking, though, about Wilma's contrast between story and physics, and I thought that every false theory the cops have is physics, and the only true one is story. A bad theory of any case is just physics trying to be a story. I wasn't sure whether or not to be proud of myself of being so smart or ashamed of myself for being so bizarre.

Dez, too, decided to weird out. She knocked the little box of chamomile bags off the counter and started to play with it. First, she pushed it around like it was a hockey puck or soccer ball. Then she grabbed it between her two front paws and began to roll on the cracked linoleum with it. She was putting on a show.

Little did I know then, but she was also showing her genius.

My cell phone rang. It had been a long time, and I no longer had the caller's ID in my register. But I knew the number all right. I answered my old mendacious comrade.

"Hello, Roger."

"Hi, Jeremy."

"Well, Roger, to say I'm surprised to hear from you is the proverbial understatement. What can I do for you?"

"I thought you'd be surly, Jeremy. I called to tell you something. I could have, probably should have, gone through channels and let it be known officially; maybe called Baxter instead of you. But I decided to relay my information this way."

"What information?"

"Information that's no big deal. I guess if it had been a big deal I would've had to go through official channels. But I don't think it is."

"The suspense is killing me, Roger." I should have said the whole phone call was killing me. When your partner bumps off a businessman and makes it look like self-defense so that he can steal said businessman's wife, and then gets a promotion job in Aurora, Illinois; and when he gets away with it by lying with consummate finesse to everybody, including me, you can't hear his buttery voice again without getting a shake or two.

"Well, OK. Here goes, Jeremy. We got ourselves a victim of unlawful means here in Aurora, guy named Frank Bunting, around 50. He got himself discovered in the alley behind the Paramount Theater here early Thursday morning. A gent of the street found him and called us. We're early in the investigation, but..."

"But what?"

"All in good time, Jeremy. But we did a full search of his recent commercial history, and he bought himself a couple of drinks down your way at the Beloit Inn bar. This doesn't mean shit, I don't think, but I'm passing it on to see if you guys down there in River City know anything about Mr. Bunting, who is, by the way, a resident of our own fair city."

I would have hung up on him at that point. I couldn't stand him any more, and he was going real unofficial on me, and I thought he had some ulterior motive for calling—like trying to get some dirt on my beloved Mary, who doesn't return my passion but who as his ex was a victim of his—extracurricular passion, that is. Dez was still determined to kill the chamomile tea box. That told me somehow: don't hang up on this lying bastard quite yet.

"When was Bunting in the bar here?"

"Credit card records show him there on Sunday night."

"This Sunday night?"

"Uh, yeah. Of course, Jeremy."

I remembered the last time Roger was in this house. I had nothing for a mixer for his drink but chamomile tea, so I made him a hot cham and gin. He took it. He was drinking a lot then. He'd take anything that had booze in it. In fact, that tea bag had come from the same box Dez seemed determined to destroy. Was she telling me something? What?

"All right, Roger. This Mr. Bunting was at the Beloit Inn center for potable delights on Sunday night."

"Yeah, Jeremy. You always had a way with words, college boy."

"And Bunting lives in Aurora?"

"Yeah, of course."

"What does he do for a living?"

"Accountant and notary. Got a sleazy rep, too."

"And the Aurora police, of which you are valued member, have naturally searched his domicile for leads."

"Yeah, we would, wouldn't we?"

"Where you are calling from, Roger?"

"My house. Why?"

I started to ask him which knee Gloria Drabble, whose husband he legally killed, was sitting on.

"You're not at the station, but I assume you have a computer of some kind there."

"Yeah. Of course."

"Would you do me a favor, Roger? This is a professional favor I'm asking for. But it'll come through channels anyhow, so we can save time by doing it right here."

"Yeah?"

"Go to your computer files and check out the inventory of what you found in Mr. Bunting's house or apartment. You do make inventories after searches in Aurora, right? You don't just do gambling down there?"

"Of course we do." Roger was huffy.

"OK. Good. I'm relieved at your virtue, Roger. Now check your inventory and see if you spot a light blue suit hanging in Mr. Bunting's wardrobe closet. Wait! How was he dressed when you found him? Was he shot to death?"

I could sense that Roger was tapping on a keyboard. He said, "Answers: Found in jeans and yellow sports shirt; shot to death, yes. Blue suit, yes. It's in the records of the search."

"Light blue?"

"Doesn't say. I can ask."

"I predict that if there's a blue suit there, or even if there's more than one, you'll find a lighter color of blue. I'd even describe it as powder blue. And have you yet located the Raven .25 he was shot with?"

"What? How'd you know it was a Raven .25? Jeremy: you're one odd dude, but you're sort of a genius."

"I'm not a genius. But Dez is."

"You and that goddamned cat."

"I'll keep you posted on developments down here, Roger. Or Baxter will do so. Why did you really want to call?"

"To say I'm sorry, Jeremy."

"You didn't need to call me to say that, Roger. I know you're sorry—as sorry as you can be."

I ended the call and gave Dez a high octane hard-g Angela meat stick. It was the least I could do for a reward. By now she'd stopped killing the chamomile box. She didn't need to any longer. She'd convinced me, by attacking the source of Roger's last drink in this house, to hear him out. I'm glad I did. I knew then that I'd been right. Our old idea of the case was just physics.

But a brand new story, a much more deadly one, had taken its place.

21: *Will Curiosity Kill the Cop?*

I was so thrilled, and frazzled, after talking with Roger that I forgot to ask him to send me a photo of the late Frank Bunting. That whole conversation was one of those moments we all have, I guess, when something signals us: "You may think you've gone onto another plane of existence, but don't worry: you're still on this one." I remembered what Abe had said earlier that day about the telephone poles in Belvidere: that they look different from the ones in Beloit and you think maybe you're doing some sort of out-of-body thing, but they're still telephone poles, so you know you're in the same old shit.

And I was sniffing the familiar feces of old, but still, I was in a new sty, and I was excited, let me tell you. I was too excited.

Roger could have easily emailed me a photo of Bunting, or I could have called him back to ask him to. But fortunately I didn't have to. Bunting was a one-man shop in Aurora, and his bushy blonde hair and moon face and zillion dollar beam were in full color on the web. The richest guy in Aurora must have been Bunting's dentist. I printed it off as Dez, now exhausted from having beaten the chamomile carton for the world's feline weight championship, watched me from the floor with one leg stretched and one eye open. I went into some cop files, entered the password, an got myself another visage altogether, and I printed it out, too. I was armed with two sheets of paper, each containing a likeness of a fellow traveler on the planet. One of them would be traveling *with* the planet, but no longer traversing upon it; while the other one was still above ground and likely stinking all the way up to the ionosphere.

I'm always a little astonished about myself when this sort of thing happens. I'm an idiot and then I see everything plain. I thought I saw everything clear now. I had been looking into darkness and thinking it was sunlight. Now I was seeing in glorious transparency, face-to-face. Well, I was unless, of course, I was just screwing up again, this time in a different way and this time without Abe and Baxter to help me lose my way—lose *our* way—in this blind man's bluff game that's otherwise known as policing.

It seemed like it should have been midnight, but that was only because the day had been full, what with our voyage to Barrington and our visits with Mendacious Margaret and Jiving Jake and our overlong drive back when Abe decided the street people in Belvidere might look like Martians compared to the ones in Beloit and then home to watch Dez assault a cham box and receive Roger's Twilight Zone phone call. That's a lot, but it was only 8 P.M. And (I'm glad you asked), I do think Roger's call was in his mind a nothing burger and that he'd only made it as an excuse to apologize to me for committing cold-blooded murder and getting by with it, and fibbing to all of us because he wanted to be known as a hero and desired a move to a bigger city and wished to have Gloria Drabble—an aging cheerleader who played mediocre cello—all to himself. I even speculate that by now he was getting tired of Gloria and perplexed that he'd only been able to trade on his staged elimination of Gloria's admittedly shoddy husband by getting to a job in Aurora when he'd wanted it to be his native Milwaukee all along.

Well, I say you can get Wittgenstein wrong in Beloit just as well as you can in Milwaukee. And I don't accept Roger's apology. He's an evil man.

Still, he'd given me more info than he realized; and hey, maybe in spite of myself I was going to do him a favor: I was going to solve Frank Bunting's murder for him. He didn't say so, Roger didn't, but I'm sure he and the force down there figured that if Bunting were really as sordid as he was purported to be, there'd be no end of people who might try to erase him. Of course I had no idea why they'd left him in the alley behind the Paramount Theater. I only knew that someday I'd like to see the Paramount Theater, which is a 1930s art deco Gothic job with fake ivory and ebony materials and funny-shaped arches and stream-lined looking curves. It's the sort of monstrosity that's purported to look beautiful, and the city of Aurora had the good sense not to tear it down, and so now it's on the national register of historic places and a great venue for Martina McBride concerts.

They'll never put up a historic plaque in the alley that says, "Here in 2017 was found the body of Franklin Bunting, crooked notary public."

Well, by now I was bidding farewell to the fatigued champion Dez and promising her a trophy one day if I came back alive; and I lumped myself into the semi-impotent blue Mazda and headed for the Beloit Inn Bar and Restaurant. It was a busy Friday night, and I figured on an excellent chance that Mr. Arthur Simpson would be on duty, showing denizens to their tables and asking the cooks where in the frigg was the caramel salmon that Table Number 18 had been waiting on for far, far too long. Mr. Simpson wouldn't appreciate my interrupting him. But I thought my business wouldn't take too long. And, like I say, I had my ammo: my two precious sheets of paper, each with a picture imprinted thereon. I even had my trusty Glock, but it was in the backseat hidden by a yellow bedspread. I was tieless but not coatless, and I was a cop. I had every right, officially and sartorially, to be inside the Beloit Inn eatery.

I parked and found Simpson right at the reservation table. It was like in the movies. He was right there. He wasn't busy. He was waiting for me. Roll 'em!

He wasn't glad to see me, and he had about him that "I'm just a slightly more intelligent-than-average kid from Rock County, Wisconsin, who despite my less than imposing looks has landed a job with rather important duties, and it's not my fault that I was the fill-in bartender that night, so

168

why don't you guys stop trying to drag me into a bloody homicide?" His whole attitude was defensive and explicitly surly. And I guess, as Mr. Softee, I'm not his idea of a Rambo cop. But, yeah, let's go back to an office an get this over with. That was good. The light back there was better— none of your indirect lighting so that people can't see their Beef Wellington. So I fished out my two documents, each more precious than diamonds or rubies to me.

And I handed them to him. And I got two grumpy "Yeahs," one for each piece of paper. Those two "yeahs" meant that I had cracked the case.

But now there was this other little problem. I had cracked the case, but would the case crack me? I shouldn't have tried to find out that night. But I'm not a cat-lover for nothing. Curiosity had me in its vise; except that I'd be going up against something far more lethal than a chamomile tea box.

22: *A Celebratory Visit in Roscoe, Illinois*

I practically skipped across the parking lot to the puny blue Mazda and headed south. There's a lot to be said for the Rockford suburbs, for both historically significant Rockton and even Roscoe in its plastic elegance. I was headed for the latter, and to the Town House Apartments on North Lomond Avenue. I wasn't sure my man lived there any more, but People Search records showed he lived in unit 119.

Before I go on with my account of this decisive moment, which the media got mostly wrong, I need to say that I had gotten lucky but I'd also made some luck, too. Fate is a peculiar thing. I have no doubt that if it hadn't been for his former treachery, Roger would never have called me with what he thought was incidental information. So you might say that in order to solve this case I had to get betrayed by a partner as mendacious as Abe was honest. But then, whatever else I am (fat, neurotic, foolish in my academic pseudo-endeavors), I've got a good memory. And I've got some intuition. The first time I talked with Arthur Simpson, the day before our trip to Barrington, I had a feeling that the key to the mystery lay in that interview and that somehow that little conversation was like the stolen letter hidden in plain sight because no one will look for it there.

It didn't take me long to find the Town House Apts, and this has nothing to do with my directional instincts and everything to do with the flat and dulcet tones of Australian Alice, whom I've made the voice of my G.P.S. Nor did it take me a lengthy period of time to sum up the Town Hall units as your typical suburban super-sized motel style apartment complex. I looked up on this starry night—when was it going to cool off, by the way—and saw a door with 219 emblazoned thereon with cheap fake-gold numbers. It was a reasonable inference that 119 was just below it. Good. I wouldn't have to climb any stairs. And before you ask, yeah: I took my Glock along. Put it in the inside pocket of my sports coat: the blazer inside the blazer. I wasn't going to need it. This was just a courtesy call. Oh, and I texted Abe: *I've cracked it, Brother. Meet me at 3215 Lomond Avenue, Rockton, Town Hall Apts 119 if you can. On my way there now.* I wasn't sure he could come. I wasn't sure he'd get the message. It was Friday night, for the Lord's sake.

I said this was a courtesy call, but really it was an announcement. I wanted to proclaim to someone that I'd solved the crime, all by myself, with a little accidental help from my lying ex-partner. I also wanted to confess—not just announce and celebrate. I wanted to confess that the whole Angel Museum had been a bait-and-switch from the gods but that we'd all fallen for it. I wanted to have a little festival for myself, a little party for myself, in Apartment 119. And why not have it with the man who fired the deadly weapon?

I wanted to throw a little party for myself as the person who is no longer deceived; no longer made a fool of by chasing angels for clues.

My pride was as swollen as my gut, which is a nicer way of saying that I was an utter imbecile.

I banged on the door. I figured: If he doesn't live here any more we might as well find out immediately.

"Accedere!"

What did this mean? I knew the guy was Italian-American, though, and the word sounded like it meant "come in" or something, so, so, so I went in.

"Jerry Ricciardi?"

"Yo."

He was sitting on the couch with the TV on: Shopping Network. And I thought: He's looking to spend his ill-gotten gains as a hit man.

"You don't know me. My name's Jeremy Dropsky, from Beloit."

Ricciardi was a very slight man with outsized shoulders. He had on a blue work shirt and brand-new jeans off the rack. What is it about blue in this case? He had luxuriant chestnut hair that spilled down his back in a tail, well secured by a rubber band or three. He had a moon face; gigantic eyebrows; a goatee, miserly lips pouting like the ass end of a goose.

"You're a goddamned cop."

"No, no. Nothing like that, Mr. Ricciardi. I'm just a sort of drop-in acquaintance."

"A cop."

As I got a little closer I first began to note that Jerry had a pair of dilated pupils. He was looking right at me but glassily away from me, too. Clammy skin shook with some jazzy blend of hyper-energy and exhaustion. His right leg from knee down was doing a jig all its own. His inhalations were at the shallow end of the pool. Jerry was with us, but you had the idea that in a little while he would only be with himself.

He seemed too far gone in OD Land for me to think he was perilous.

"No, I just dropped in, Mr. Ricciardi, to say that I too like the bar at the Beloit Inn. Maybe we could meet there sometime. I'm sure I can find a powder blue suit to wear; I go to Goodwill all the time. I'll have a few and head out into the midnight air where the sweet Rock River flows; take a gentle amble down the bike and walking trails; and end up dead in front of a museum dedicated to the uplifting spirit of angels. That's angels, Mr. Ricciardi, not angel dust."

"You're bunk-o. I don't know you. I don't like you. See, I don't like you."

"I can't see why, Mr. Ricciardi. Say, that's a nice glass table you got over there. Is that a water pistol? I like them when the barrel is silver, don't you? As I live and breathe, I believe that's a Raven .25. I like how the barrel sort of cranes its neck out of the handle, like its squinting its eyes for a powder blue suit to shoot. I'll bet that gun's not color-blind, not even at midnight last Sunday."

"You're a cop, and you're a fat cop and you got a fat lip."

"Yeah, well, right on all counts, Mr. Ricciardi. I'll be on my way, however. There's just one thing I don't know. Who tipped you off to the powder blue suit? I'm sure it's the guy who paid you off. You screwed up. Good help is hard to find. But you made up for it, probably in Aurora, and now you got all the bling-bling you need in this world, right? Is that the Shopping Network on? I like to keep the volume down low, too. Say, look at that turquoise ring. You can afford that now."

I averted my gaze just long enough to admire the ring, which happened to be that Friday night's HSN special. Somehow he crossed the ten feet to the glass table whereon the Raven lay in all its world-destroying majesty. This required an almost overtaxing effort for a man as far gone as Jerry was. By the time he returned to the couch, Raven in right paw, you'd have thought he'd run the four-Bminute mile. This man was sufficiently removed from La-La Land to sense that he was in many kilos of trouble. He was hopped up and a lot more threatening than I, in my determination to have a celebratory announcement of my deductive triumph, had thought. I was really good at remembering how a substitute bartender casually mentioned a guy with a ponytail. I was real bad at avoiding the predicament that could get my chubby ass shot off.

"Hey, Mr. Ricciardi. There's no need for gunplay here. Yeah, I'm a cop, but I'm an out-of-town cop. There's no need to fire in anger at an out-of-town cop. We guys just head back to where we came from and never get seen or heard from again."

"You'll be back, man. But I'm gonna put you on your back."

I thought at that point—I who was bathed in a tremolo sweat—that he might not be competent enough in his near-overdosed condition to plug me. I thought it might be ready, fire, aim. I felt my Glock warm against my upper torso, an old friend who said, "If I could help, you know I would." If Dez had been there, he'd have turned this gun-toting turkey into a ripped up chamomile box. But Dez wasn't there. This guy had the drop on me. I thought: The guy probably killed in the wake of a heroin deal, but he's made the mistake of touching too much of the merchandise. I knew that I was going to hear a loud report, a deafening crack in that small apartment space. I hoped that was the worst of it—that I'd just go temporarily semi-deaf. I think, I can't be sure, that I closed my eyes. It was like when a preacher baptized me once. He plunged me beneath the tank but before that I shut my eyes so it wouldn't seem so scary. Was I about to be christened by a Raven .25?

I heard the crack of a pistol, like a jet had broken the sound barrier in Apartment 119. I heard a clang. Then I opened my eyes and saw blood gushing out like a fountain. It was like one of those horse races: you know, a signal and then they're off; except it was the blood that was off. The gusher didn't last long, and the clang was the sound of a Raven .25 striking a faux teakwood floor in Rockton, Goddamned Illinois.

"He was about to air condition you, Brother."

I leaned, knees and legs warping fast, against the gray panel wall by the door. Mr. Ricciardi was moaning in authentic gangster gibberish and strumming his red right hand on the strings of a non-existent banjo. To ward off pain, shake vigorously.

"I don't know. Maybe he was bluffing."

"You could have fooled me, Brother," said Abe. "Are you aware of how little authority you have in the Land of Lincoln?"

23: *An Idiot's Summary*

"Don't know about you, but I spell 'idiot' D-R-O-P-S-K-Y," said Charlie Baxter.

It was Monday morning, and we were all back at hindquarters. I started to say, "Well, Charlie, you may say I'm an idiot, but the Sunday papers are saying I'm a hero. Abe and I are heroes. The Rockford paper said, BELOIT COPS CAPTURE MURDER SUSPECT AT GUNPOINT, while the Janesville paper said, TWO BELOIT OFFICERS SEIZE HOMICIDE SUSPECT. I noted Janesville was a little more restrained. Maybe they didn't want to upset the Cuppses over on Columbus Circle—they had enough category 1 hurricanes in their lives already. Anyhow, I didn't remind Charlie that Abe and I were heroes. I just said:

"Yeah, Charlie. I know I am an idiot. Abe here saved an idiot." Actually, I wasn't totally sure Abe had saved me. Ricciardi might not have been able to shoot straight, but this is just college boy skepticism talking. Ricciardi had killed two guys the way you or I might fire a staple gun and he was way up in the heroin stratosphere and I'm a great big target. Yeah, Abe likely saved Mom and Pop funeral expenses. Well, maybe the department would have paid.

On the other hand, I had had a few fantasies. I was shot but not killed; went on disability; went back to Beloit

College; studied philosophy; learned to read Wittgenstein. Yeah, I had such thoughts. What's wrong with me?

"Why would you even go down there, Dropsky?"

"Well, Charlie, I should have gone through channels. And, look, I'm not a heroin addict like our friend Ricciardi, he with the temporarily defective paw, but I get a little high on myself sometimes. And I just wanted to tell somebody that I'd cracked the thing, and I thought why not tell the perp, OK?"

"Even if you'd gotten out of there without Woodruff's help, the perp might have fled. You were warning him."

"No, no, no. I didn't warn him. I teased him. I never accused him of anything. Did I?" This wasn't strictly true.

"Well, you were there, Jeremy. We weren't."

"Oh, yeah. Well, I just wanted to celebrate a little and shake him up a little. I had no idea I would be visiting with a total hophead."

"Roscoe cops are unhappy. You should have called them and explained what you knew and let them take it from there."

"They're just jealous."

Abe said, "Well, Charlie Baxter. Brother Dropsky and I are heroes for a day. The guy's in custody. We can add attempted murder to the books. All has ended well, as Jesus Christ and General Jackson have long ago decreed."

"You have a wonderful way with the mule puck, Abe," said Charlie. "OK, enough. Tell us, Dropsky, you idiot, how you came to break this thing open. Start with how you ID-ed Ricciardi."

"Well, when I learned from Aurora that the recently-offed Bunting was in the bar that night, I thought back to the little side interview I had with Arthur the Bartender and I remembered him mentioning a guy in a ponytail. Ricciardi is the only hit man I know in the Stateline that has a ponytail. I knew him only by rep of course. The story is he does work for bag men out of Rockford who need some muscle when a drug deal goes down towards Antarctica. His day job he packs boxes for a discount warehouse. I just thought that, if Bunting was the sort of guy bad guys would want to hit, and he was in our very own River City bar that night, and if a guy with a ponytail was also there, Ricciardi would be that guy. And I was right."

"Well," said Charlie glowering. "And here I thought this was about the Angel Museum somehow. I'd say Jerry Ricciardi flunked angel school a long time ago."

"We all three got into this thing wrong in a couple of ways. First, we thought the Angel Museum locale was important. Second, we treated the D.A.G. and the Woodstock Raven pistol as evidence, when it was really just a coincidence. We cops don't believe in coincidences, and that's because we're on the hunt for perps. But coincidences happen a lot. And that's all this was. Maggie Bryce called her husband a devil in angel's clothing or garb, and her new sleaze-o lover's brother had a Raven stolen. But the phrase about a devil posing as an angel is common. And Ravens are common, too. It's no surprise that the phrase and gun just happened to come together in the guise of the merry widow and her greasy hunk."

"Impressive, Brother Jer. Where'd you get all this stuff?"

"From a college teacher"

"Well," Abe followed up, "at least you didn't get it from your cat. We're making progress here."

"Very funny, Abe. My sides are splitting or hadn't you noticed?"

"Go on," said Baxter. He was losing patience with us both.

"Well, we all three drew the wrong inference from the bartender's memory of the powder blue suit. He said he was sure he recalled Jon Bryce in the bar that night because there were two guys in powder blue suits. He more or less said that if only one powder blue suit had been there he'd not have even noticed the suit or remembered the guy wearing it. He only noticed, he said, Bryce wearing one because another guy was wearing one there, too. We treated the adventure of the two blue suits as a memory trigger for Art the Bartender. We totally missed what was really going on with those two light blue suits."

"What do you mean?"

"OK. Well, before I answer that, let me just say that there are lots of powder blue suits in this world, but what are the chances that two of them show up in a little bar in Beloit,

Wisconsin? This seems to be much less a coincidence that the devil/angel business and the Raven."

"So it wasn't a coincidence—these two blue suits?"

"Actually, Charlie, they were. But this time it was a really important coincidence."

"Can't you get to the point, Jeremy?"

"Yeah, right. Well, Charlie, the point is that Mr. Ricciardi was in the bar, too, that night, packing a Raven. Art the Barkeep remembered his ponytail. And why was Jerry, that great solid citizen, there? He was there doing his sacred professional duty as a hit man. And his target was one Frank Bunting of Aurora, Illinois. Mr. Bunting is an accountant and notary who got into the moral universe all wrong. He had a rep for notarizing shady bills of sale: you know, the sort of thing that says this is for a purchase of safety pins when it's really a purchase of highly illegal drugs. But dealers and kingpins like these fake pieces of paper; they're tokens of 'I paid you, so you'd better deliver.' It's sort of what they do for legality. Well, Bunting would notarize these and jack up the price for doing so. Now as to why he got targeted, and by whom—who was paying Ricciardi—I don't know. My guess is that Bunting was not keeping his mouth shut and maybe shuttling between kingpins with valuable information. And I think Ricciardi was hired by someone with resources because, among those resources, was someone who could track Bunting all the way to Beloit, to the Beloit Inn, and someone who could call Jerry

Ricciardi up and say, 'He's in the bar and he's wearing a light blue suit. Can't miss him!'"

"You're saying Ricciardi saw two powder blue suits—a coincidence, right, Brother—and shot the wrong guy; plugged the wrong light blue suit."

"I am, Brother Woodruff. And why? Well, Bryce was sitting near the back while Bunting was sitting at the bar. This is what Arthur told us. I think Ricciardi thought, 'the guy sitting at the back: he's the scared one. The guy at the bar: Bunting must know he could be killed, so Bunting wouldn't be sitting out in the open at the bar. Ergo, Bunting must be the guy hovering near the back of the bar.' Well, why was Bunting sitting at the bar? Maybe because he didn't think he was in any danger, or maybe because if he sat at the bar with other people around the shooter would be less likely to strike, at least in the tavern. We'll never know. We just know that Ricciardi shot the wrong powder blue suit. He was targeting Bunting and hit Bryce."

"Why in front of the Angel Museum? Why would he move the body there?"

"You just won't give up on the Angel Museum angle, Charlie. We thought there must be drag marks but the rain washed them out. There probably never were drag marks. Ricciardi left Bryce in front of the Angel Museum because that's where Bryce was when Ricciardi found him. I guess Bryce was touring the facades of new museums in the old hometown. He fell there around midnight, but no one saw him there until early light. Roscoe cops found a silencer in Jerry's apartment, and that muffled the noise. Nobody found him until the dawn's early light because poor Jonathan was wearing a powder blue suit. He wasn't wearing a glow-in-the-dark yellow suit."

"So the day Bryce decided to put on his powder blue suit on Sunday was the day he sealed his fate."

"Yeah, Charlie, and that should be a lesson to us all. Beware of what you wear. Try to think like a hit man."

"You're being funny, Jeremy."

"Yeah."

"But," said Abe, "what was Bryce doing in Beloit? He hadn't been in his hometown in elephant's years. And did Ricciardi shoot Bunting in Aurora behind the Paramount?"

"Oh, I think Bryrce was just passing through. We need more info from Chicago on that. Or..."

"Or?"

"He'd decided it was time to apologize to his brother, whom he snaked at Ripon College years ago."

"Why do you think that?"

"Oh, I don't know. September just seems to be National Apology Month or something."

"And my other question?"

"Well, I'm sure Aurora cops will want to converse with Mr Ricciardi about the unlawful death of Mr. Bunting. There's a gentleman of the constabulary down there named Roger Webb. You may have heard of him. He's the one who told me Butning had been at the bar on that fateful evening."

"Will Ricciardi flip and tell us who hired him?" This was Charlie.

"I don't know. What do you think, Charlie?"

"I think he won't flip, Jeremy. If a big pin hired him and he turns state's evidence, they'll ice pick him in prison. He'd rather take his chances with the state and keep his mouth zipped."

"Wouldn't the state if Wisconsin put him in protective custody?"

"Protective custody?" said Charlie. "Come on, guys, this is max security prison we're talking about here: max security for the public, not the prisoners."

24: *No Heroes Allowed*

A few weeks passed, and tree colors began to hit peak yellowish brown. Every now and then the sun caught the top of the oak outside my window and lit up the gorgeous procession of its temporary death. The oak would not rise again, arrayed in all its glorious green, for six months, if then.

Apparently Jerry Ricciardi was stupid enough to use only the one gun. His Raven was traced via ballistics to the demise of both Jonathan Bryce and Frank Bunting. Charlie figured that whoever hired Jerry told him he had to make up for his error in Beloit by rubbing out Bunting in Aurora—and that no, there wouldn't be any extra money for the added hit. So we had solved our case and Roger's case, too.

But Jerry was not interested in any conversation. He was no doubt offered a plea deal locally, but drug lords have long arms, and he figured a shorter sentence for a guy who'd opened his trap would also be a death sentence inside the walls. So he declined to say who'd hired him and said he was motivated by personal grudges (unspecified) against Jonathan and Frank. No one believed him. He also said, earlier, that the Raven belonged to a cousin (also unspecified) and that it was he, and not Jerry, who fired it fatally. Later he said it was he, Jerry, who did it, but that's about all he would say. Well, at least we got one bad guy off the avenue. Drugs would continue to flow like all the streams that contribute to the mighty Mississippi—something that our very own local Rock River is guilty of, with the scene of the crime down in the Quad Cities.

As the days passed the media finally got a more accurate picture of Abe's and my heroics, by which I mean that it realized that Abe was the real hero. I got a supporting role, and they hushed up the fact that I had no business ever dropping in on the sky high Jerry in the first place; but it was Abe who rescued me and who called the ambulance to take the trembling and miserable Jerry away, where his wound was diagnosed as poignant, yes, but in the end only a flesh wound. It grazed Mr. Ricciardi's digits just enough to make him drop his piece. A precise shooter Abe Woodruff is.

Finally, in late October Abe's pastor proposed that the church have a celebration for Abe and me. Abe was a parishioner, while I am a heathen. But the good Lord had delivered us both, and He had also sent Abe off to shoot me out of trouble—actually, I thought it was my text message that did, but The Good Lord (henceforth: TGL) might admittedly have been working through it. So the idea was to have the usual church service but then dedicate the reception afterwards to the major hero and the minor one. The pastor even said that Abe and I could invite whomever we wanted, as long as we made it clear that they shouldn't just come for the party but also for the preceding service.

"How about it, Brother?" said Abe after he apprised me of this offer.

"Sure. It's been a while since I went to church, and I'm betting the goodies at the party will be free. I'm not against religion, Abe, as long as folks don't think the soul is a thing, like a dog or a bedstead."

"What? Of course the soul is thing. I've got one, and you've got one."

"Not according to Wittgenstein."

"Jeremy, do me a favor. Just give me a yes or no about the idea."

"Yes."

"Good man. I'll tell Pastor Wynn. He thinks you're a hero, you know."

"He's wrong, but I'm sure he knows a lot about the Bible."

The event was set for the first Sunday in November. A motley assemblage gathered at the little tabernacle, and we sang together about

How happy are the saints above
That once went sorrowing here.
But now they taste unmingled love
And joy without a tear.

I had wanted to bring Dez along, especially to the reception, but was told no. I didn't necessarily want to bring her to the service. I knew that Pastor Wynn wanted Dez to know the gospel, but he also knew that he knew not her language. Yet Pastor Wynn did know *our* language. He spoke with a shouting beauty about love: "Our Lord Jesus showed us the way: put God first, others second, self last. Our friend Abe, and our special guest Jeremy, put each other first. Brother Abe was guided by God, whom he put first, to help out Brother Jeremy. If they had put self first, they would not be here to celebrate in joy with us today."

This was not strictly accurate. I had put myself first, and that's why I went gloatingly and stupidly down to Roscoe in the first place. I wanted to give myself a fete for being so clever. That's because I have so little else, outside Dez: heavy, college drop-out, unloved by my treacherous ex-partner's wife. Pastor Wynn was wrong: I *was* putting myself first. It was Abe who put me first. He could have ignored that text. God in a way *did* lead him to honor it and show up. Pastor Wynn went on:

"The poet who said that we must love each other or die was literally right when it came to Abe and Jeremy. Had they not loved one another, at least one of them would have died. Love isn't just a nice idea, my friends. Love *works*."

At the end we sang:

I've anchored my soul
In the haven of rest.
I'll sail the wild seas no more.

The tempest may sweep
O'er the wild, stormy deep.
In Jesus, I'm safe ever more.

After multiple announcements (the Missionary Union won't meet tomorrow afternoon), we gathered in the reception hall—homey, concrete basement floor notwithstanding—for cake and punch. I've never tasted better cake. The coconut icing had a slightly tart sweetness, and the cake itself was golden moist and firm at once. Abe and I decided to invite various and sundry people, including Skip Bryce and Rose and her hated Susan. We also invited that swinging Columbus Circle couple the Cuppses, but we never heard back from them. They were bit players, and dysfunctional to boot, so we should never have asked them in the first place.

Needless to say, Margaret Bryce and Jake Abernathy were not invited and wouldn't have attended. They must have been glad to be cleared, and now they could stew freely in their own juices. I had had a dream about them, in which Dez sprouted angel's wings and flew to Barrington. There she spied upon Meg and Jake and reported back to me that Jake was a disgusting fellow, in bed and out, but Meg seemed devoted to him. "Go figure," said Dez in her special meow dialect. I did. I tried to go figure.

But I failed.

At the church party Skip Bryce walked up to me. His hair had turned whiter, but he was no more rodent-like than he was before, poor guy. He bent forward in that faux aggressive way of his. His voice had gotten raspier.

"I was happy to be dropped out of the list of suspects, Jeremy, and I'm glad you and Abe are all right. Of course this is my brother we're talking about here, and while we were at odds for years, he's still my brother and he met a pretty awful end."

"I don't know how long he lingered. Not long, I think, Mr. Bryce. I hope not anyhow."

"What in hell could he have been doing in Beloit?"

Here I had a decision to make. Jonathan's Chicago associates had finally gotten back to Charlie. Jonathan had lots of business irons in the fire, including a cut-rate new exercise bike, and he'd been on the road. The day of his death he'd been finishing up some business in Indianapolis with a Sunday brunch. He was on his way to Des Moines. No doubt he got tired of driving and decided to make Beloit an overnight rest stop. He likely had a little curiosity about how Beloit had changed and so chose the Beloit Inn downtown. I knew all this, and yet I said:

"Oh, I think, Skip, he might have been planning to drop in on you."

"You think so?"

"Sure, why not? Maybe he wanted to make amends. Maybe he wanted to apologize for all those years ago when he tripped up you and Margaret at Ripon."

No."

"It's possible. If I were you, Skip, I'd try to believe that. It'll make Jonathan's death more holy for you. [I think Pastor Wynn was starting to get to me.] It'll be a lot more sacred than something like 'my brother was an ass, and he was in the wrong place at the wrong time and wearing the wrong suit.' If you think he was here to apologize, then his death in front of an Angel Museum will seem appropriate to you."

"I'd never quite thought of it that way, Sergeant."

"Well, do."

"By the way, what was all this business about finding that woman who called me for an insurance quote. I heard some gossip that you tried to tell the other policemen that that was a good alibi for me. But Jon was killed later."

"My colleagues on the force look at everything through physics."

"Physics? I got a C+ in that at Ripon. Was always pretty good at math but never at science. Go figure. Anyhow, what do you mean by physics?"

"Well, Mr. Bryce, it's hard to explain. But I just knew that a guy like you, with such a cock-eyed alibi that turned out to be true, would never plug your brother to death. It's not strictly logical, unless the heart has its own logic. It's narrative, not physics. I'm not sure I can explain it better. Anyhow, I turned out to be right."

"That you did, Jeremy; and I appreciate it."

At this point Elizabeth Woodruff joined us, tiny and swaying in a pleated dark green dress. She said, "Just for the record, Jeremy, I think you and Abe are equally heroes."

Elizabeth always had a way of putting me on the back heel. "Why?"

"Well, because if you hadn't bumbled your way down to Roscoe, Abe wouldn't have had anybody to save."

"Oh."

Skip said, "By the way, Jeremy. I know you interviewed Margaret. I guess she's happy to be in the clear, too. How is she? Do you know?"

I didn't want to reveal to Skip that his old love was now bathing in a rusty tub of grease with the words "Jacob Abernathy" on the label. It might break his heart. So I said, "Not really, Mr. Bryce. Abe and I just interrogated her. I suspect Mrs. Bryce just needs a good leaving alone for a while—you know, so she can grieve." My internal chuckle at that remark was surely not audible.

But I think Elizabeth heard it. She said, "Grief is always exceeding the speed limit," and walked away. Enigmatic Elizabeth never failed to be herself and was forever leaving me without any syllables of my own. Abe knew how to communicate with his lovely wife. I did not.

But hey, at least I could talk to Dez.

I was surprised that Rose and Susan had decided to show. Abe and I thought that Rose with her incessant plaints about her half-sister, and her almost lethal efficiency around the office, deserved an invite. Rose was even pushing Susan in her wheelchair. Had Pastor Wynn's love feast gotten to them, too?

Abe said, "It's good to see you two. Now remember: it's Sunday, so no fighting."

"Actually," said Susan in the chair, "we've made up for a while."

"Jesus Christ and General Jackson," said Abe. "How did that happen?"

"Well, Sergeant Woodruff," said Rose in her outsized auburn and pink tent, "it wasn't really a miracle. We just figured out one day last week that the problem all along was our dad. He was driving when Susan was injured, and he wanted to blame me because he wasn't paying attention to the road. He was just trying to clear himself, and in order to do that, he'd set Susan and me against each other by claiming that it was worry about me as a teen that led to his lousy driving."

"Wait a minute, you two," I said. "You mean that it's not Pastor Wynn's sermon on love that changed everything. It's that you found a common enemy?"

Susan bristled. She banged a fist on the black rubbery arm of her wheelchair. She was as pathetically thin as Rose was pathetically obese. There was a terribly unwelcoming skeletal quality to Susan's appearance—not that I'm all that magnetic myself.

"That's a very mean way of putting it, Jeremy Dropsky."

"Sorry, Susan. Well, Abe and I are just really glad you could make it. Can I fetch you some more punch?"

Actually, I had made this offer, which was accepted, because I saw in the bare corner of my pudgy eye what I had been dreading. Mary Webb was chatting with the man whom, as rumor and Abe had it, was the new man in her life. This was the associate pastor, Roy Beasley. He was tall and blonde, with a near crew cut on top. He wore a slightly preppy blue blazer (no, not powder blue but navy blue) and brown khaki trousers and a blood red tie with bright orange crosses stitched thereon. He smiled with obvious adoration at Mary, who remained ensconced in the boyish haircut that I found irresistible and the pretty round face, at once wholesome and exotic, that was the chief thematic motif of my soporific fantasies. Ray Charles's "Making Believe" reverberated in my soul (which is not a thing, by the way), and I especially recalled Ray's lyrics: "You've got somebody new. You'll never be mine."

The way to avoid this happy duo was to keep moving: keep fetching new red punch for the newly reconciled Susan and Rose. But as I was making my delivery of same, Mary cried out: "Jeremy! Come over here. I'd like you to meet Roy."

Mary, like Jerry Ricciardi, had the drop on me.

"Just a moment, Mary."

I gave Rose and Susan their refills and entered the lion's den.

"Roy, I want you to meet Jeremy Dropsky. Jeremy used to be Roger's partner."

"I'm pleased to meet you." I extended a well-padded hand.

"Likewise, Sergeant. Many blessings. We're so glad we could have this event for you and Abe. Congratulations on your heroism. God bless."

Roy had a presence that was very masculine and very oleaginous at once. He was like firm butter. These pastors seem to have a patent on this recipe. Why would Mary go for something like this? Why would Margaret Bryce go for a oily bastard like Jake? Why would Roger go for a fourth-rate cellist and outmoded homemaker like Gloria Drabble? Why will no one go for me?

"Well," I said, "it was really Abe who was the hero. He got me out of a situation I should never have put myself in. And," I added a little sneer of protest against my successful rival lover Roy, "he's the religious one."

"Anyhow, Sergeant Dropsky," said Roy, "this is a wonderful day the Lord has made."

"I'm glad you're a hero, Jeremy," said Mary with a sort of shy anger. "But I've got some mixed feelings about heroes."

"What do you mean?"

"Well, Roger always wanted to be a hero. And then he became one. And then he left me. So, Jeremy, I'm glad you're a hero. But I'm not sure how much I like heroes."

"Oh, " I said, the tears of injury glistening on my soul. But the soul isn't a thing. Wittgenstein said it wasn't. I wondered what Dez was getting up to about now. I hoped to see her soon.

THE END

ABOUT THE AUTHOR

Tom McBride is co-author with Ron Nief of *The Mindset Lists of American History* (Wiley, 2011) and *The Mindset List of the Obscure* (Sourcebooks, 2014). He has authored as well four mystery novels (*Godawful Dreams, Rox & Darlene, The Homicide At Malahide* and *The Curious Old Men of Belial College*). *Godawful Dreams* was featured on public radio's Chapter A Day during summer of 2016. He is also author of *The Great American Lay: An All Too Brief History of Sex,* and *When You Could Only Dribble Once: 51 Famously Forgotten Game-Changers*, which features among others Beloit College's great coach Bill Knapton. His most recent works of mystery fiction are *Bent Dead in Beloit, The Jaded Lady of Janesville, Wisconsin, That Bad Old Baylor Corpse* and *Bill Shakespeare, Sports*

Writer. His most recent book is *Thank Your Mother's Boyfriend for Dying Young: How the Liberal Arts Can Reduce Your Pain.*

Elizabeth Freeman and Art Robson deserve my thanks for their contributions—all credits theirs; all debits mine.

Made in the USA
Columbia, SC
21 April 2022

59280514R00109